THOMAS HARDY

The Woodlanders

Retold by Margaret Tarner

Founding Editor: John Milne

Macmillan Guided Readers provide a choice of enjoyable reading material for learners of English. The series comprrises three catergories: MODERN, CLASSICS and ORIGINALS. Macmillan **Classics** are retold versions of interbationally recognised literature, published at four levels or grading – Beginner, Elementary, Intermediate and Upper. At **Intermediate Level,** the control of content and language has the following main features:

Information Control
Information which is vital to the understanding of the story is presented in an easily assimilated manner and is repeated when necessary. Difficult allusion and metaphor are avoided and cultural backgrounds are made explicit.

Structure Control
Most of the structures used in the Readers will be familiar to students who have completed an elementary course of English. Other grammatical features may occur, but their use is made clear through context and reinforcement. This ensures that the reading, as well as being enjoyable, provides a continual learning situation for the students. Sentences are limited in most cases to a maximum of three clauses and within sentences there is a balanced use of adverbial and adjectival phrases. Great care is taken with pronoun reference.

Vocabulary Control
There is a basic vocabulary of approximately 1600 words. Help is given to the students in the form of illustrations, which are closely related to the text.

Glossary
Some difficult words and phrases in this book are important for understanding the story. Some of these words are explained in the story, some are shown in the pictures, and others are marked with a number like this: … [1]. Words with a number are explained in the Glossary

Contents

A Note About the Author

Thomas Hardy was born on 2nd June 1840, at Higher Bockhampton. This small village is near Dorchester, in Dorset – a county in the south of England. Hardy's parents were poor, working people.

Thomas went to a school in Dorchester and he studied Latin, French and German as well as literature, science and art. At the age of 16, he began studying architecture. When he was 22, he went to London and worked for an architect. He returned to Dorset in 1867, and in the same year he began to write his first novel. At this time, Hardy fell in love with Tryphena Sparks. Their romance continued during the summer of 1869 until, in 1870, Hardy went to work in the county of Cornwall. There, he met Emma Gifford, the daughter of a rich lawyer.

Hardy's first novel, *Desperate Remedies*, was published in 1871. Between 1871 and 1895 he wrote 15 other novels, some short stories and poems. In 1874, Hardy married Emma Gifford, and he stopped working as an architect. He and Emma went to live near Dorchester in 1887. Hardy designed their large house himself. He called it Max Gate.

Hardy became rich and famous and many important visitors came to meet him at Max Gate. But his marriage to Emma was not happy. When she died in 1912, the writer was very upset and from that time he wrote no more novels. Instead, he wrote poetry. Many of his poems were sad.

Most of Hardy's novels were about the countryside and the people in the south-western counties of Dorset, Devon, Cornwall and Hampshire. Hardy called this area Wessex, a very old name for this part of England. Some of Thomas Hardy's most popular novels are: *Far From the Madding Crowd* (1874), *The Return of the Native* (1878), *The Mayor of Casterbridge* (1886), *The Woodlanders* (1877), *Tess of the d'Urbervilles* (1891) and *The Trumpet-Major* (1880). Films have been made of many of Hardy's books.

Thomas Hardy married his second wife, Florence Dugdale, in 1914. They lived quietly in Max Gate. Hardy was given honorary degrees from Oxford and Cambridge universities and the Gold Medal from the Royal Society of Literature. He died on 11th January 1928. His body was buried in Westminster Abbey, in London. His heart was buried in a small churchyard in Dorset.

1

Little Hintock in Winter

It was a cold winter evening in 1855. Most of the people of Little Hintock had stopped work for the day, and they were all in their homes. It was late, but lights were shining from the windows of a few of the houses and cottages.

The village of Little Hintock lay in a small valley near the edge of a large area of woodland. There were trees of many kinds in these woods – oaks, elms, ashes, hazels[1] and many others. The people who lived in the little village earned their living[2] from the trees.

Every kind of tree had a use. Big old oaks were cut down and their thick trunks were sold. The timber was used for building houses and for making furniture. The timber from the hazel trees was used to make hurdles[3] for fences and for thatching[4] roofs.

Between the village and the woodland there were apple orchards. The apple trees had a use too. Their fruit was used to make cider. The villagers drank some of the cider them-selves and they sold the rest at the market at Sherton Abbas. Sherton Abbas, which was ten miles from the village, was the nearest town.

In front of one of the cottages in Little Hintock, there was a tall elm tree. On this winter evening, light was shining from the windows of this cottage, and from its open door. It was late, but inside the cottage a young woman was working. She worked by the light of a small fire and of one candle.

The young woman wore a leather apron and she had a big leather glove on her left hand. In this hand, she held a long piece of hazel wood. With a heavy knife, the woman cut the wood into four thinner pieces. She sharpened the ends of each piece into a point. These thin spars were used by thatchers. There was a great pile of spars by the girl's feet.

After a while, the girl stopped for a moment and put down her knife. She looked at her right hand. It was red and sore. Then she picked up the knife again and started to cut another piece of hazel wood.

Suddenly, there was a knock on the open door of the cottage and the girl looked up.

'There's nothing here for you, Mr Percomb!' the girl said. 'I don't want to sell my hair. I've told you that before! Why should another woman have it?'

The girl's face was not pretty, but her beautiful hair was long and thick. Its colour was a wonderful red-brown. The visitor put out his hand and touched it gently. Mr Percomb was the barber from Sherton Abbas. He had never seen such beautiful hair.

'A lady wants it, and she wants it now,' the barber said. 'Please cut it off and sell it to me. You need the money, Marty. I know that your father is ill. And you only earn a few shillings[5] a week by making these spars.'

'Who is this lady?' Marty asked. 'Why does she want my hair?'

'Her hair is exactly the same colour as yours,' the barber replied. 'But it isn't thick, like yours. She wants me to make a hair-piece[6] for her. If I make one from your hair, everyone will think that all the lady's hair is her own. She is going abroad[7] soon, so no one will know the truth about it.'

'Ah! Then I know who she is!' Marty said. 'She's Mrs Charmond, who lives at Hintock House! She sat behind me in the church on Sunday. Well, I'm not going to sell you my hair. Why should *she* have it?'

'Because she's rich and she wants it,' Mr Percomb said with a laugh. 'And remember this, Marty South – this cottage is part of the Hintock House Estate[8]. The owner of the estate

6

Her beautiful hair was long and thick. Its colour was a wonderful red-brown.

also owns this cottage. Mrs Charmond can make you and your father leave your home whenever she wants to.

'Now listen to me, Marty,' the barber went on kindly. 'Here are two gold sovereigns. I'll leave them here, on this table. Cut off your hair and bring it to my shop in the town tomorrow. Then you can keep the money!'

Marty shook her head. 'No! I'm not pretty, but I'm not ugly either. I'm not ugly because I have beautiful hair. Why should I make myself ugly for Mrs Charmond? She can find a new husband without any help from my hair!'

The barber smiled. 'I didn't say anything about husbands,' he said. 'I think that you're looking for a husband yourself, Marty South.'

Marty blushed[9]. Then she turned away from the barber and she began her work again.

After Mr Percomb left, Marty ran upstairs to her father's bedroom. John South was an old man. He was sitting in a chair near the window. His eyes were closed.

'Father,' Marty said quietly, 'can Mrs Charmond make us leave this cottage?'

John South opened his eyes and looked at his daughter.

'No, the leases[10] on this cottage and Giles Winterbourne's house are lifeholds. While I am alive, nobody can make us leave this cottage and nobody can make Giles leave his house. You are safe here until I die, Marty. But that won't be long now. I know that I shall die soon!'

Suddenly, the old man looked at the dark window.

'That old elm tree out there will kill me soon,' he said. 'It will fall on the cottage and kill me in my bed.'

'That's nonsense, Father,' Marty replied. Then she went downstairs and began working again.

'Mr Percomb was wrong,' she said to herself. 'Mrs Charmond can't make us leave. I shall keep my hair!'

8

Soon, all the other cottages were dark, but Marty went on working. The village was quiet, except for the bell of the church clock which rang every hour. A few minutes after the bell had rung for three o'clock, Marty stood up. She sighed.

'I've finished!' she said to herself. 'Now I must take the spars to Mr Melbury's shed. I thank Heaven that I am strong enough to do Father's work!'

The girl tied a woollen scarf round her head. Then she picked up two bundles[11] of spars and she walked out into the darkness of the night. She turned into the small lane which went through the village.

The wind was moving the tall trees and the night was full of strange sounds. But Marty South was a woodlander and she was not afraid of the dark. She carried the bundles of hazel spars to a long open shed, behind a big old house at the end of the lane. Then she walked back to the cottage for two more of the heavy bundles.

At last, all the bundles were in the shed. Marty stood in the lane for a moment and looked up at the windows of the house where George Melbury, the timber-merchant, lived.

Suddenly, the back door of Melbury's house opened. A middle-aged woman stood in the doorway holding a lighted candle in her hand.

'George! George! Where are you?' the woman called into the darkness. 'It's nearly four o'clock. Please come indoors!'

George Melbury moved into the light of the candle. The timber-merchant was a tall, thin man with a smooth face. He was worried.

'I can't sleep, Lucy,' Mr Melbury said. 'Why hasn't Grace written to us this week? I'm worried about her. Perhaps she's ill.'

'Things always seem bad in the night,' Mrs Melbury said. 'You'll feel better in the morning. Please come inside now, George.'

'I'm worried about Grace's future too, Lucy,' George

Melbury went on. 'I want our daughter to marry well. If she marries Giles Winterbourne, she'll be poor until I die.'

When she heard this name, Marty South listened very carefully.

'But Giles loves Grace so much. And love is better than money,' Mrs Melbury said.

'I know that Giles loves Grace,' Mr Melbury said. 'But Grace is a lady now. She's better than Giles now. She isn't a woodlander any more.'

'Then why must they marry?' Mrs Melbury asked.

'You know the reason, Lucy,' her husband replied. 'The lady who became my first wife was going to marry Giles Winterbourne's father. But I married her instead. Giles' father married someone else, but he was never really happy after that. And my first wife soon died. Everything went wrong! I've always worried about what I did. And that's why I want Grace and Giles to marry – it'll make everything right between our families.'

'Please, George, let's talk about this tomorrow,' Mrs Melbury said. Then she put her hand on her husband's arm and she led him gently indoors.

Marty South walked slowly back to her cottage.

'So, Giles Winterbourne cannot be mine,' she said to herself sadly. 'He's going to marry Grace Melbury.'

Inside the cottage, she looked at her reflection[12] in the mirror. Then she looked at the two gold sovereigns on the table and her eyes filled with tears. Quickly, she picked up a pair of scissors from the table and she began to cut off her long, beautiful red-brown hair. She did not look in the mirror again. When she had finished cutting, she wrapped the hair in some paper and she left the parcel on the table. Then she went to bed.

But Marty could not sleep. At five o'clock, she got up and she got dressed.

Soon afterwards, there was a knock on the door.

'Are you there, Marty?' a voice asked.

'Yes, Mr Winterbourne,' Marty said. 'I'm coming.'

She put on her bonnet[13] quickly and she opened the door.
She smiled at the handsome young man who stood outside.

'Mr Melbury knows about your father's illness,' Giles
Winterbourne said kindly. 'He'll give Mr South more time to
finish making the spars.'

'The work *is* finished,' Marty said. 'The spars are all in Mr
Melbury's shed. Come with me and I'll show you where they
are.'

The two young people walked to the timber-merchant's
shed, and Giles Winterbourne looked at the bundles of spars.

'Marty, I believe that you did all this work yourself,' he
said. 'And you've done it very well. But let me look at your
hands.'

He held the young woman's sore, red hands in his own
strong hands.

'Oh, Marty, you've hurt your little hands!' he exclaimed.

'Please don't tell Mr Melbury that I made the spars, Mr
Winterbourne,' Marty said. 'Help me put them into one of
the wagons now.'

Giles Winterbourne began to throw the bundles into one
of the timber-merchant's tall wagons which stood in the shed.
When he had finished, he turned and looked at Marty again.

'What has happened to you, Marty?' he said. 'Your head
looks so small. What have you done?'

'I've made myself ugly – that's what I've done,' Marty
said sadly.

'No! You haven't made yourself ugly,' Giles said with a
smile. 'But you've cut your hair. Take your bonnet off, Marty.
Let me see.'

But Marty turned and ran back down the lane towards her
cottage.

11

2

Grace Comes Home

Later that same morning, George Melbury met Giles Winterbourne in the lane outside Giles' house. The two men knew each other well. They often worked together. Mr Melbury was a timber-merchant. His busiest times were winter and spring, when the trees were cut. Giles Winterbourne was a tree-planter and a cider-maker[14]. His busiest time was autumn, when the ripe apples were pressed to make cider. So the two men used the same horses and wagons. They helped each other when they could.

'Giles!' Mr Melbury called when he saw the young man in the lane. 'At last I've had a letter from Grace. She's coming home today. She's coming in the coach to Sherton Abbas. If you're going to the market later, will you bring Grace back from Sherton Abbas? She's been living at her school in the city for a long time. She's made friends with other girls there. She has many new friends. And I expect that she has new ideas too. But you two can talk on the journey home and you can make friends with each other again.'

'I hope that she hasn't forgotten her friends from Little Hintock,' Giles said quietly.

'No, no. She's a good girl,' Mr Melbury replied. 'She'll be happy to see you.

'Grace will be in Sherton Abbas at five o'clock,' Mr Melbury went on quickly. 'You will have finished your work in the market by then. Don't go in one of the wagons. Take my gig[15]. You'll travel faster in that.'

So Giles took Mr Melbury's gig and started on the journey to Sherton Abbas. As usual, he took an apple tree with him as an advertisement. He always stood with an apple tree in the middle of the town square on market days. People who wanted to buy apple trees saw his advertisement and they ordered their new trees from Giles.

The apple tree was tied across the gig and it moved with every step of the horse. Giles was a happy man as he travelled to the market. A few miles along the road, he saw Marty South. She was going to the market too, but she was walking.

'Climb up here and ride with me, Marty,' Giles said kindly.

Marty thanked the young man and she got into the gig with her basket.

'I hope that your father is feeling better, Marty,' Giles said. 'I worry about him often, because of the leases on our homes. You know that when your father dies, the owner of Hintock House Estate will have to decide what to do with your cottage and my house. That seems wrong to me, but nothing can be done about it. I hope that Mrs Charmond will let us stay in our homes.'

Marty nodded sadly, but she did not reply.

'Today, Mrs Charmond is getting my hair,' she thought. 'And when my father dies, she'll take my house from me.'

Marty got down from the gig before they reached the market.

'It's Grace Melbury who will be with you in the town,' she said. 'Thank you for bringing me here, Mr Winterbourne. Goodbye.'

Giles did not answer, but he blushed as he watched Marty walking quickly away.

The girl went first to Mr Percomb's shop and she gave the barber the parcel of her hair. Then she went to buy some food. Soon, it was nearly four o'clock. Marty crossed the town square. She saw Giles Winterbourne standing there with his apple tree. Suddenly he looked up in surprise. Then he smiled. But he was not smiling at Marty. He was smiling at another young lady, someone who was very different from

Marty South. Miss Grace Melbury had arrived early. As she walked towards Giles, she pulled off one of her white gloves and held out her hand.

Grace was slim, with a pretty, gentle face and brown hair. Her dress was smart and fashionable. Marty took a step towards the two young people, but then she stopped.

'No, I am not wanted here,' she said to herself. 'I must go home quickly. I don't want those two to see me on the road. They won't want me to ride with them.'

Marty walked as fast as she could out of Sherton Abbas. After half an hour, she looked at the road behind her. It was getting dark, but she could see the Melburys' gig far behind her. She also saw a carriage with bright lamps, much nearer to her.

After a minute, the carriage passed Marty. Then, to her surprise, it stopped.

'Come up here, young woman,' the driver called to her. 'Mrs Charmond wants you to ride with me.'

Marty climbed up onto the carriage and she sat beside the driver. When the carriage was moving again, the driver whispered to her.

'This is very strange,' he said. 'Mrs Charmond has never stopped for a villager before. Usually, she takes no interest in the villagers at all.'

Soon the carriage was near Little Hintock. The driver stopped outside the gates to Hintock House and Marty got down onto the road.

'Good night,' said a soft voice from inside the carriage.

'Good night, Mrs Charmond,' Marty replied.

A minute later, she had turned off the road and she was hurrying down the lane to Little Hintock.

———

At first, the two young people in Melbury's gig sat silently together. Giles was thinking of the times when he and Grace

14

*As she walked towards Giles, she pulled off one of her
white gloves and held out her hand.*

had been younger. But Grace was thinking of the school friends that she had left behind in the city.

'It's good to see you again,' Giles said at last. 'It reminds me of the past. I remember the times when we used to be together. I remember a picnic in the woods, Miss Melbury. On the way home, I put my arm round your waist. Your father didn't mind – and neither did you!'

'We were younger then,' Grace replied. 'I do not think about those days now. Let me tell you what I did last summer.'

'Oh – yes,' Giles said. 'Please tell me.'

So Grace talked about her life and about her friends. Giles listened but he said nothing.

'She doesn't want to talk about the past,' Giles thought. 'And she doesn't want to talk about the future. But it doesn't matter. Her father wants us to be married. Everything will be all right.'

It was very dark now. Giles turned the gig into the lane which led to the village. Soon they stopped outside the Melburys' big old house. Light was shining out from the windows.

Grace's parents had heard the gig and they hurried out to greet their daughter. Giles helped Grace to get down and he began to follow her into the house. But Mr and Mrs Melbury had forgotten him. They wanted to talk to their daughter. So Giles walked along the lane towards his own house. No one would be waiting there for him. Giles lived alone. His mother and father were dead.

In the lane, the young man passed the Souths' cottage. For a moment, Giles thought of Marty. She was so different from the pretty, well-educated Grace Melbury.

3

A New Friend

Grace was tired after her long journey and she went to bed early. But she could not sleep. Through her window, she could see a bright blue light shining from a house on the other side of the little valley.

Grace sat up in bed to look at the strange blue light. At that moment, she heard her parents coming up the stairs to their bedroom. And after that, Grace heard the slow steps of the Melburys' servant, Mrs Oliver. The old woman was going to bed too.

Grace got out of bed quickly and opened her door. She spoke quietly to the servant.

'Mrs Oliver, come in and talk to me,' she said. 'Tell me about that strange light on the hillside.'

Mrs Oliver looked at the light and smiled.

'That's the young doctor's house,' the old woman said. 'His name is Edred Fitzpiers. He's a very clever young man. I clean his rooms every week and he talks to me sometimes. The doctor has hundreds of books in his house. And he does experiments in his laboratory[16]. That's where the blue light is coming from.'

'Why did a clever young man come here, to Little Hintock?' Grace asked.

'Well, long ago, the doctor's family lived near here,' the old woman replied. 'Perhaps he likes this place. Perhaps he feels at ease[17] here. But the people here don't trust him. He's clever, but Doctor Fitzpiers hasn't got many patients.'

'Then he will certainly go away soon,' Grace said.

Mrs Oliver shook her head.

'No, Miss Grace, he'll stay here,' she said. 'I have a secret.

17

Doctor Fitzpiers has bought my head! He gave me ten pounds for it!'

'What do you mean?' Grace asked in surprise.

'The doctor thinks that my brain is bigger than other women's brains,' Mrs Oliver said. 'He wants to examine[18] my head, after my death. If he was going to leave Little Hintock, he wouldn't have bought my head, Miss.'

'Oh! I wish that you had not told me!' Grace said.

After the old woman had gone, Grace Melbury continued to look at the light on the hillside. She wanted to meet the clever young man who was so different from the people of Little Hintock. Doctor Fitzpiers knew about the world outside the village – and so did she.

_____

Giles Winterbourne was busy all the next day. But he could not stop thinking about Grace. He was worried. George Melbury had not spoken about their marriage for some time. *Did* Mr Melbury still want him to marry Grace? Had she changed too much to marry a woodlander like Giles? Giles did not know. But there was something he did know – he loved Grace more than ever. He loved Grace and he wanted to remain friends with her father. So, that evening, Giles walked to the Melburys' house.

Mr and Mrs Melbury were very excited.

'Grace is going to Hintock House tomorrow,' Lucy Melbury told Giles. 'She is upstairs in her bedroom. She is choosing the clothes that she will wear tomorrow. I must go up and help her.'

'Grace and I met Mrs Charmond in the village this morning,' George Melbury explained to Giles. 'The two of them were soon talking together. Grace is well educated. She is as good as any lady now. She and Mrs Charmond will be friends. And that will be good for Grace.'

Then Mr Melbury saw the unhappiness on Giles' face.

18

'But that won't make any difference to you and Grace,' Mr Melbury said quickly. 'My daughter will be your wife, Giles. I am happy about that. I'll call her now. She'll want to speak to you.'

'Thank you, sir,' Giles replied. 'But Grace is busy now. I'll come again another time.'

As Giles left the house, he looked up at Grace's bedroom window. Grace had put on a pretty bonnet and she was smiling at her reflection in a mirror.

———

The next morning, Grace Melbury walked happily towards Hintock House, the home of Mrs Felice Charmond. The house was half a mile from the village. There was a lane which led to Hintock House from the main road to Sherton Abbas. But there was also a path which led to the house from the village. Grace walked quickly down this narrow path through the woods. She had never been to the big old house before. She felt excited and a little afraid.

Soon Grace saw Hintock House in front of her. It stood in a hollow[19] in the woods. There were green lawns and tall trees around the house and green ivy grew thickly over the front of the house. Hintock House was beautiful! Grace walked up to the front door and rang the doorbell.

A servant took Grace to a room where the owner of the house was waiting. Mrs Charmond smiled at Grace and walked towards her.

'My dear, I am so happy that you have come,' Mrs Charmond said. Then she led Grace along a gallery filled with beautiful paintings and furniture. At the end of the gallery, there was a small table with teacups and a teapot on it.

'Let us both have a cup of tea,' Mrs Charmond said. 'Sit down, my dear.'

Mrs Charmond leant back in her chair.

She led Grace along a gallery filled with beautiful paintings and furniture.

'Will you pour the tea, please?' Mrs Charmond said in a soft, slow voice. 'I really cannot move much today.'

'I am very sorry that you are ill,' Grace said quickly. 'I hope that I shall be able to help you.'

'I am not really *ill*,' Mrs Charmond replied. 'But I always feel tired in this house. I am happier when I am travelling in Europe. I love travelling, Grace. I would like to write about my travels. But when I am here, I am too tired to write. My dear, perhaps you could write down my ideas for me.'

Grace was very surprised, but she was pleased.

'If I can help you —' she began.

'I am sure that you can,' Mrs Charmond said. 'You are a clever, well-educated girl. Perhaps you write books yourself? Does anyone write books in Little Hintock?'

'Well, I do not know, Mrs Charmond,' Grace replied. 'But a doctor is staying here now. I believe that he *reads* many books. Perhaps he writes books too.'

'Ah, yes, the doctor. I have heard about him,' Mrs Charmond said quietly. 'Do you know his name?'

'His name is Edred Fitzpiers,' Grace replied. 'His family used to live at Oakbury Fitzpiers, which is a village near Sherton Abbas.'

Mrs Charmond was silent for a few moments. Then she smiled.

'I knew someone called Edred once,' she said. 'Well, we need a doctor here in Little Hintock. Is he old or young? Have you seen his wife?'

'I do not think that he is very old and he is certainly not married,' Grace replied. 'But I have not seen him.'

The two women talked for an hour or two. Mrs Charmond was very kind to Grace. The young girl was happy to have a new friend. Now she knew someone who could talk about books and about people from outside Little Hintock.

When it was time for Grace to leave Hintock House, Mrs

Charmond walked with her to the door. They stopped for a moment in front of a big mirror. Mrs Charmond looked at Grace's pretty young face and she looked at her own reflection in the mirror. Her own face looked much older than Grace's, and she was not happy about that. But when she said goodbye to Grace, she promised to invite her to Hintock House again very soon.

———

That same morning, Giles Winterbourne had been thinking often about Grace. He was not happy about Grace's visit to Hintock House.

'Her friendship with Mrs Charmond might take her away from these woodlands and away from me,' Giles thought. 'But her home is here, in Little Hintock. And her father wants us to be married. How can I make Grace more interested in me? What can I do? Yes! I know – I will invite Grace and her parents to a Christmas party!'

At that moment, Giles heard someone knocking at the front door of his house. He opened the door.

Marty South was standing outside the house.

'Why didn't you come to the plantation, Mr Winterbourne?' she asked. 'We must plant a hundred young fir trees today. Had you forgotten about them? I've been waiting for you in the woods.'

'I'm sorry, Marty, I'm afraid that I *had* forgotten,' Giles replied. 'I'll come with you now.'

Giles Winterbourne loved working with trees. Every tree that he planted grew healthy and strong. He often paid Marty South to help him. Marty loved trees too.

That morning, the two young people were working in a new plantation. This part of the wood was next to the lane. There was a low holly hedge between the plantation and the lane.

They worked hard. Giles dug holes in the ground. Then

Marty held each little fir tree in its hole while Giles spread out the roots and pressed earth around them.

Giles was soon warm from the hard work of digging. But Marty was not moving very much. She got colder and colder. After several hours, she could not hold the trees any more.

'Mr Winterbourne, can I run to the village? I want to warm my hands and feet,' she said.

Giles looked at her.

'You're cold because you cut off your hair, Marty,' he said kindly. He laughed. 'Run home and get warm.'

Giles was happy to be alone for a while. He had remembered that Grace would be returning from Hintock House soon. She would be walking along the lane.

Marty ran home to her cottage. And a few minutes later, Giles saw Grace on the other side of the holly hedge. But as he moved towards her, he saw another young man looking at Grace. This young man was standing in the woodland on the other side of the lane. He was handsome and well dressed. When he saw Giles, he turned and walked quickly away. Giles knew that this man was Doctor Fitzpiers, but the two of them had never spoken.

Giles pushed through the holly hedge to meet Grace.

'You've been to Hintock House,' Giles said. 'That's why you look so happy! Did you like Mrs Charmond?'

'Yes, she was very kind,' Grace replied. 'But she does not like our winter weather. She plans to go abroad soon. She wants me to go with her, Giles! She wants me to write about her travels. She knows a lot about books. She likes French books best. We had a very interesting conversation about them.'

'Did you, Miss Melbury?' Giles said. 'I don't know anything about French books. But I can plant a tree better than any other man in Little Hintock.'

'And that is much more important,' Grace said with a

23

smile. 'I love Little Hintock and everyone in it, Giles. But I *would* like to travel with Mrs Charmond.'

'Well, Miss Melbury, you must ask your father about that,' Giles replied. They walked on together to the Melburys' house, where they said goodbye. Giles said nothing about his Christmas party, or about his hopes for the future.

Later, he returned to the new plantation. Marty soon came back too and she helped him to plant some more trees.

'If a man wants a friend to be interested in him,' Giles said to her, 'should he invite the friend to a Christmas party? Would that help him?'

'Will there be dancing at the party?'

'Well, yes. There might be dancing.'

'And will the two people dance together?' Marty asked.

'Well, yes, I think so,' Giles replied.

'Then the party might help him,' Marty said sadly. She did not ask Giles who his friend was. She already knew the answer.

———

Later that day, Giles went to the Melburys' house. The women were not at home, but Giles spoke to George Melbury.

'Will you and your wife and Miss Melbury come to my house for an hour, the day after tomorrow?' Giles asked the timber-merchant.

'I can't answer you now,' Mr Melbury replied. 'I must ask Mrs Melbury and Grace. Grace is used to good society[20] now.'

But that evening, Mr Melbury spoke to Grace and his wife.

'Giles wants us to go to his house for an hour, the day after tomorrow,' he said. 'I think that we *should* go.'

The women agreed. Mr Melbury sent a message to Giles the next morning.

4
The Party

Giles Winterbourne was planning a big party. He invited all his friends from Little Hintock. On the morning of the party, the house was completely cleaned and lots of food was prepared.

At about four o'clock, Giles was in the bakehouse[21], next to his kitchen. He had made a big fire under the oven. There were lots of pies on plates, next to the oven. They were ready to be cooked. Inside the sitting-room, a boy was cleaning and polishing the furniture[22].

Suddenly, Giles heard a noise and he looked up. To his surprise, the Melburys were walking towards the bakehouse. They were very smartly dressed.

'My dear Giles, I see that we have made a mistake about the time of your party,' Mrs Melbury said.

'You are going to have a big party!' Mr Melbury said, as he looked around. 'There is a lot of food to be cooked! Shall we go home and come back in two hours?'

'No! Please stay,' Giles said quickly.

'If we stay, then Lucy and I will help you,' Mr Melbury said.

'And I will help too,' Grace said.

'No, *you* mustn't do anything, Miss Melbury,' Giles replied.

So Mrs Melbury and her husband helped him, while Grace watched them.

———

Very soon, the food was in the oven. And soon, Giles' other guests arrived. Everybody went into the sitting-room and drank tea.

25

'You are not used to village parties now, Miss Melbury,' Giles said to Grace.

'No, you are right!' Grace replied. 'But I like this party and I like your house, Mr Winterbourne. Nothing has changed in Little Hintock. I wish that I had not got polish from this chair on my dress. But it does not matter. The dress is not new.'

Grace smiled. But Giles was unhappy. Everything was going wrong.

————

Soon it was time for the meal. The food was put on a big table. Giles brought the pies from the bakehouse. Creedle, a villager who helped Giles with his business and took care of the house, came into the room. He was carrying a big pot of stew. He poured the hot stew into a large dish on the table. Suddenly, Grace gave a cry and put her handkerchief to her face.

'Good Heavens, the hot stew has splashed onto you!' Giles exclaimed. 'Why did you do that, Creedle?'

'It does not matter,' Grace said quickly. But her father frowned[23] at Giles, and the poor young man was even more unhappy.

'I shouldn't have invited Grace and the villagers to come here together,' Giles thought. 'Grace is not used to village society any more.'

After supper, there was dancing. Some musicians from Sherton Abbas had come. They played lots of popular tunes. But Grace had been away in the city for a long time. She had learnt new dances there, and she had forgotten the old village dances. So she did not dance with Giles or with anyone else.

After the dancing, an old woman spoke to Grace. She wanted to tell the young woman's fortune[24].

'I'll tell you about your future, my dear,' the old lady said.

'Grace doesn't believe in fortune-telling!' George Melbury

26

said angrily. 'She is an educated woman now!'

The Melburys were the first people to leave the party.

'Well, Giles is a good man,' Mr Melbury said to his wife when they were alone. 'I sent Grace to a good school because I wanted to make her a good wife for him. But her education has changed her. She doesn't want to meet village people now. That's not the kind of society she's used to.'

'Grace will soon get used to life in Little Hintock again,' Mrs Melbury said.

'But will life in Little Hintock be good for her?' Mr Melbury said.

———

Two weeks went by. Grace did not meet Mrs Charmond again. She was not invited to Hintock House again. Melbury could think of only one reason – Mrs Charmond had heard that Grace had been at Giles Winterbourne's party. She thought that Grace was only a village girl. She was not good enough to be the friend of the owner of Hintock House!

One evening, Mr Melbury was sitting in his office. He called to Grace to come and talk to him.

'Sit down, Grace and look at these,' he said, pointing to some papers. 'These will be yours one day. They are worth a lot of money. Perhaps if Mrs Charmond knew about them, she would invite you to her home again. That money and your education will give you a place in good society.'

'But I am engaged to marry Giles Winterbourne, Father. I will not have a place in good society. I will stay here, in the village. I will be a woodlander.'

Mr Melbury sighed[25]. At that moment, old Mrs Oliver came to tell them that their meal was ready. And she had some news.

'Mrs Charmond is going abroad tomorrow,' she told them. 'She'll be away from England for the rest of the winter.'

'Well, you've lost your new friend, Grace,' her father said.

'She heard that you were at Winterbourne's party. I am not happy about this. Don't meet Giles again without telling me!'

'I never meet Giles,' Grace replied quietly.

'That's good!' Mr Melbury said. 'You couldn't live happily with him now. You must end your engagement to him.'

Grace sighed, but she did not reply.

———

That evening, two of the villagers were also talking about Giles Winterbourne. Creedle, who helped Giles, was talking to a friend.

'Marty South's father is very ill,' Creedle said. 'When old Mr South dies, Mr Winterbourne will lose the lease of his house.'

'Then Mrs Charmond will own Marty's cottage and Mr Winterbourne's house,' the other man said. 'She will be able to do what she likes with the properties!'

As the men were talking, Giles was standing in the garden of his house, thinking about his future. He knew that he might lose his home when Mr South died. He was worried. Suddenly, he saw Marty South running towards him.

'Oh, please come to my father, Mr Winterbourne!' Marty said. 'He's so worried about that old elm tree in front of our cottage. He's sure that it's going to fall and kill him!'

Giles followed Marty back to her cottage. They went upstairs to John South's bedroom.

'Ah, Mr Winterbourne, that elm tree is going to kill me,' John South said. 'You'll lose *your* house when I die.'

'Don't think about that,' Giles said. 'I'll climb up the tree tomorrow afternoon and I'll cut off some of the branches.'

'But Mrs Charmond won't let you to do that!' John South replied.

'She will never know about it. I won't take the tree away,' Giles told him. 'I'll only remove the most dangerous branches.'

———

The next afternoon, Giles returned to the cottage with a ladder[26] and a sharp saw[27]. Soon, he was cutting branches from the tree. It was misty and dark by about five o'clock. Inside the cottage, Marty and her father were watching Giles through a window.

Suddenly, Giles saw Grace Melbury walking along the lane.

'Miss Melbury! Good afternoon!' he called.

Grace looked up, and she saw Giles working in the tree. But she did not reply. She was still thinking about her father's words. She did not want to disobey him. She walked quickly past the South's cottage.

But Grace was a kind girl. She did not want to be rude to Giles.

'What shall I do?' Grace whispered to herself. Then she turned and walked back to the elm tree.

'Giles – Mr Winterbourne,' she said. 'I have something to tell you. My father thinks that we should forget about our engagement. But we can still be friends, I am sure of that.'

'I don't know what to say, Grace,' Giles replied. He was surprised. 'I must think about this.'

'Perhaps I *will* marry you one day, Mr Winterbourne,' Grace told him. 'But we must not think about it now.'

Giles said nothing. But he stopped his work and covered his face with his hands. Grace waited at the bottom of the tree. But Giles did not move, and he said nothing more.

After a moment, Grace walked sadly away.

About fifteen minutes later, Giles finished what he was doing. He climbed down from the tree and went home.

————

The next morning, Giles was too busy to think about his troubles. He was helping Mr Melbury that day. There was a heavy load of oak trunks to be taken to a town many miles away. The huge tree trunks were tied to a wagon with big red wheels. Four strong horses were pulling the heavy load, and every horse wore bells. The morning was misty. It was impossible to see very far. But other drivers on the road would hear the horses' bells. They would move to the side of the road and wait for the long timber wagon to pass.

Giles Winterbourne walked beside the timber wagon. The horses walked slowly through the village. They pulled the wagon along the lane and they turned onto the road towards Sherton Abbas. Suddenly, Giles saw the lights of a carriage coming through the mist towards the wagon.

'Didn't you see our lights?' the carriage driver shouted. 'You must turn your wagon!'

'No. I won't turn. It will be much easier for you to turn,' Giles shouted. 'We've got four horses and a heavy load.'

'But there's another carriage behind me,' the driver of the carriage said. 'We are travelling to Italy.'

'I'm sorry. *We* couldn't see your lights through the mist, but *you* must have heard our bells,' Giles replied. 'You must turn your carriages.'

Then a woman's voice called from inside the first carriage.

'Why have we stopped? I'm in a hurry!'

But Giles would not turn his wagon. At last, the carriage drivers turned their carriages and drove them onto the grass by the side of the road.

The wagon moved slowly on. Giles walked beside it. As he passed the first carriage, a woman leant out of the window. She had beautiful, thick, red-brown hair.

'Who is that rude, unpleasant man?' the woman asked the driver of her carriage.

'That's Giles Winterbourne, from Little Hintock, Mrs Charmond,' the man replied.

Giles heard the man's words. He was angry with himself. He had upset Mrs Charmond. He knew that George Melbury would be angry with him.

30

As he passed the first carriage, a woman leant out of the window. She had beautiful, thick, red-brown hair.

5

The Writing on the Wall

The next morning, Giles Winterbourne took from his desk all the legal papers about the leases on his house and the Souths' cottage. He read the papers carefully.

Giles' mother had been a member of the South family. She had bought the leases on the two properties from the Hintock House Estate, many years before. When she died, the lease of her house passed to[28] her husband, Giles' father. The lease on the other property – the cottage – passed to her relation, John South.

Giles found a paper from the Estate's lawyer.

While John Winterbourne and John South are alive, they and their families may live in the properties. And when one of the two men dies, nothing will change. Both families may continue to live in the properties. But when the second man dies, both the leases will end. They will end one month after the death of the second man. The properties will belong to the Hintock House Estate again. The leases will not pass to the families of the two men, John Winterbourne and John South.

Giles' father had been dead for some years. So when John South died, all the property would belong to Mrs Charmond.

With the papers about the leases, Giles found a letter addressed to his father. It was from the lawyer for the Hintock House Estate. It had been written several years after the other paper.

To John Winterbourne

The Hintock House Estate agrees that if you want to continue the lease of your house for the life of your son, you may do this. You must pay a fee of twenty pounds, and you must sign this letter and return it to me.

'Why didn't my father pay the fee and sign the letter?' Giles asked himself. 'But it doesn't matter. John South is still alive. I will pay this money to the lawyer now, and then the house will be mine. Mr Melbury will be happy if I have a good home for Grace. Perhaps I *will* marry her one day.'

Giles put the papers in his desk and he went to see John South.

Marty opened the door of the Souths' cottage. She looked very unhappy.

'Father is even more frightened of the elm tree now,' she said. 'He says that it looks taller and more dangerous with fewer branches. He says that it could fall on the cottage at any moment!'

'Well, what can I do, Marty?' Giles asked.

'The tree is making Father ill,' Marty replied. 'The doctor says that it must be cut down. He is upstairs with Father now.'

At that moment, Doctor Fitzpiers came down the stairs.

'That tree must be cut down today or tomorrow, or your father will die,' the doctor said to Marty.

'It's Mrs Charmond's tree,' Giles said. 'We must ask her permission before we cut it down. And she is in Italy.'

'A man's life is more important than a tree!' Fitzpiers replied. 'Cut it down early tomorrow morning! The old man will not see it fall. Then he will not worry any more.'

———

That evening, Winterbourne helped two other woodlanders to cut halfway through the trunk of the tall elm tree. Then,

33

very early the next morning, they completed their work. Soon, the old tree lay on the ground.

Fitzpiers returned to the cottage a few hours later. He went upstairs with Giles. Marty had already dressed her father and the old man was sitting in his chair as usual. Giles pulled back the curtains. He pointed through the window.

'Look, Mr South, the big tree has gone,' he said.

John South looked through the window and saw the empty sky. He went very pale and he gave a terrible cry.

'Oh, it's gone! It's gone! Now I must go too!'

They were the old man's last words. He died a moment later.

'Well, my advice has killed him!' Fitzpiers said. 'I did my best.'

After a few minutes, the doctor and Giles went downstairs.

'Who was that young lady that we were both looking at in the woods?' Fitzpiers asked Giles with a smile.

Giles looked at the doctor, then he walked away without a word.

———

George Melbury soon heard about old Mr South's death. He knew that it might make problems for Giles Winterbourne.

'I'm sorry for Giles, Grace,' Mr Melbury said to his daughter. 'But you're lucky. You're not his wife.'

'I pity[29] Giles,' Grace said sadly.

'I'd like to help him,' Mr Melbury said. 'Giles will always be my friend. He can never be your husband and my son-in-law now. But I don't want him to lose his home.'

———

'This is very difficult for you, Giles,' Mr Melbury said to the young man, when he met him the next day. 'You must write to Mrs Charmond. Explain everything to her. Tell her about the letter which your father didn't answer. Perhaps she'll let

34

you pay the money now. Then you could stay in the house for the rest of your life.'

'No. I don't want to write to Mrs Charmond,' Giles replied. 'I don't like her, and she doesn't like me.'

'But you *must* write to her, or to her lawyer, Giles,' Mr Melbury said. 'It's important for your future.'

So Giles sent a letter to Hintock House. The servants there sent it on to Mrs Charmond in Italy. By this time, everyone in the village knew about Giles' problem. Everyone hoped that Mrs Charmond would be kind to him. Grace and her father were nearly as worried as Giles himself.

Every day, Giles waited for the postman. And one morning, he got a letter from Mrs Charmond's lawyer.

Some of the other villagers came to Giles' house to hear the news. They watched the young man open the letter. He read it quickly and then looked up.

'It's not good news, friends,' he said. 'Mrs Charmond is going to have my house pulled down. I must leave the house within a month. I curse her!'

That afternoon, Giles spoke to George Melbury again.

'A few months ago, I bought this quiet, grey horse,' he said. 'I call the horse Darling. I wanted to give it to Grace when we got married. But I can't keep it now. Will you take it to her?'

'There is something I must say to you, Giles,' Mr Melbury replied. 'Soon, you will not have a house. You will not have a home for Grace to live in. You must not think any more about getting married to her.'

'I still want Grace to have this horse,' Giles said.

'I will buy the horse from you, and give it to my daughter,' Mr Melbury said sadly.

Giles did not say any more. He went back to his house and he thought about Grace and about her father's words. He wanted to know about Grace's own plans. Did she agree with

'A few months ago, I bought this quiet, grey horse. I wanted to
give it to Grace when we got married.'

her father? He wanted to ask her. He decided to meet her if he could. But he did not believe that she still wanted to marry him.

That evening, the woodlands and the village were quiet. Suddenly, Giles heard a strange noise outside his house. It was a scraping noise. Giles picked up a candle, but before he reached his front door, the noise had stopped. The young man went outside. He held the candle high in the air. Some words had been written on the white wall of the house. They had been written with a piece of burnt wood.

Oh Giles, you've lost your dwelling-place,
And now, dear Giles, you'll lose your Grace.

'Well, that's true,' Giles said to himself. 'I must stop hoping that she will marry me!'

Giles went back into the house and wrote a short letter.

Dear Mr Melbury
I agree with you. My engagement to your daughter has now ended.
Giles Winterbourne

Although it was late in the evening, Giles took the letter to the Melburys' house at once. No lights were shining from the windows. Everyone was asleep. So Giles put the letter under the door and he walked quietly home.

———

Early the next morning, Grace went for a walk. Her father had not yet told her about Giles' letter. As she walked past Giles' house, she saw the writing on the wall. She was angry. She did not want other people to make decisions for her.

Giles was in his garden, talking to one of the villagers. Grace thought that he had seen her. She picked up the piece of burnt wood, which was lying by the wall of the house. She crossed out the word 'lose' and wrote the word 'keep' above it.

'Giles saw me here. He will guess that I did that,' Grace said to herself. 'Father is wrong. I think that we *should* get married.'

Grace walked in the woods all morning. But later in the day she saw her father and she spoke to him seriously.

'Father, I have made up my mind,' she said. 'I do not want to end my engagement to Giles.'

Her father was very surprised.

'You are talking nonsense, Grace,' he said. He gave her Giles' letter. 'Read this!' he said.

Grace read the letter without speaking.

'Giles must have written this after he had seen me change the writing on his wall,' Grace thought. 'I can do nothing more.'

———

Giles knew who had written the words on his wall. And he had seen the change in the writing. But he had not seen Grace outside his cottage. That morning, Marty South came to the house. She was going to work with Giles again.

'Marty, why did you write those words on my wall last night?' Giles asked her.

'Because they were true,' Marty replied.

'Then why did you change them this morning?' Giles asked.

'What do you mean? I didn't change them,' Marty said. She looked at the writing again.

'One of the village boys must have done it. The words are nonsense now,' Marty said. She picked up the piece of burnt wood and she crossed out all the words.

6

'Pity is not Love'

Doctor Fitzpiers was a little afraid of the woodlands. He was not a woodlander, he came from a big town. He did not like to drive through the woods when it was dark.

One evening, the doctor was driving home in his gig. Two miles from the village, he saw Giles Winterbourne walking along the road. Fitzpiers stopped the gig.

'Come up here and ride with me,' the young doctor said.

Giles got into the gig, and Fitzpiers began to talk at once.

'Is there a young lady staying in the village – a pretty girl, very smartly dressed?' Fitzpiers asked Giles.

Giles said nothing, but he knew that Fitzpiers was talking about Grace.

'She is not a woodlander, I am sure of that,' Fitzpiers went on. 'But she cannot be staying at Hintock House, because Mrs Charmond is away from home. I have only seen the girl two or three times, but I cannot forget her!'

'Are you in love with the young lady?' Giles asked quietly.

'Oh, no!' Fitzpiers replied. 'But I would like to know who she is. An unmarried man is often lonely in a country village!'

By this time, Fitzpiers was driving through Little Hintock and they were near the Melburys' house. Giles saw lights shining from the window of Grace's room. Then Grace herself came to the window. She began to pull the white curtains across it. Suddenly, the doctor saw her too.

'There she is!' Fitzpiers cried. 'What *is* she doing there?'

'It's her home,' Giles replied quietly. 'Mr Melbury is her father.'

'Is that true?' the doctor asked. 'Is that beautiful, well-dressed young woman the timber-merchant's daughter?'

'Money can buy anything,' Giles said with a laugh. 'Why can't a village girl who is clever and pretty look as good as a lady? You know who she is now. Do you like her less?'

'Well, perhaps I like her a little less,' Fitzpiers replied. 'But she is pretty, very pretty!'

'Yes, she is pretty,' Giles replied sadly.

————

Later that evening, Grace was in Mrs Oliver's bedroom. The old lady was ill for the first time in her life. She was ill, but she did not want Doctor Fitzpiers to examine her. She told Grace why.

'The young doctor paid me ten pounds for my head. I told you that, Miss Grace. He wants to look at my brain after my death,' the old woman said. 'When I took the money, I thought that I'd live a long time. But now I'm ill and I'm afraid!'

'How can I help you?' Grace asked kindly.

'I want you to go to the young doctor. Tell him that I don't want to sell him my head. He'll listen to you. But I've already spent two pounds of his money and I can't repay it.'

'I will give you the two pounds,' Grace said. 'And I will speak to the doctor for you. Please do not worry any more.'

————

The next morning, it was raining heavily. Grace left the house very early. She did not tell anyone where she was going.

Fitzpiers was looking out of his bedroom window when Grace came into his garden. He saw her and he hurried downstairs to open his door to her.

'I will not come in, Doctor Fitzpiers,' Grace said. 'My name is Grace Melbury. I have come with a message from Mrs Oliver. She is my father's servant. You made an agreement with her – about her head. She has made a decision. She does not want to sell her head. So I have brought back

40

your money.'

Fitzpiers looked at Grace for a moment. Then he said, 'Please come in, Miss Melbury. Your clothes are very wet.'

Fitzpiers led Grace into his sitting-room and he took a piece of paper from his desk.

'Here is my agreement with Mrs Oliver. Please take it,' the young man said kindly. 'And tell the old woman to keep the money.'

The doctor smiled at Grace.

'Do you think that it was a strange agreement, Miss Melbury?' he asked her. 'I am a scientist, as well as a doctor. I am interested in unusual things. I am interested in experiments. I work in my laboratory every night.'

'I know that, Doctor Fitzpiers,' Grace said. 'I have seen the lights shining from your window, late at night. I think that your work is very interesting. You are very clever. I admire you very much!'

Fitzpiers smiled happily. Grace Melbury admired him! And *he* was admiring Grace's pretty face and her sweet smile. He continued to think about Grace after she had left.

'I cannot *marry* her,' Fitzpiers said to himself. 'One day I will marry a rich, beautiful woman. But I will enjoy the friendship of this pretty girl while I live in Little Hintock. She will make country life more pleasant for me.'

———

Spring came early to the woodlands that year. Soon, the trees were covered with new green leaves, and flowers began to appear everywhere.

One afternoon, Fitzpiers was walking in the woods with a book in his hand. He was in a part of the woodland where most of the trees were oaks. Fitzpiers was going to sit down under one of the oak trees, but then he heard a strange noise. He walked towards the place where the noise came from.

It was the 'barking season' in the woodlands. Soon,

Fitzpiers came to a place where many of the woodlanders were working. They were removing the bark from the trunks of trees which had been cut down. Fitzpiers recognized Marty South and some of Melbury's workmen. The young man walked closer to them. As he watched them, George Melbury drove up in his gig, with Grace beside him. Mr Melbury saw Fitzpiers and invited him to stay for a simple meal with the workers.

Everyone stopped working. Someone lit a fire and Marty South made tea in a big pot. Edred Fitzpiers was happy. He looked at Grace and at the woods around him. He was not frightened of the woods in the daytime!

'This place is beautiful – and so is Grace Melbury!' he thought. 'Perhaps I *could* be happy here with her.'

He walked over to Grace and began to talk to her.

When they had finished their meal, the woodlanders began to go to their homes. The Melburys went away too. Only Fitzpiers stayed on, sitting near the fire. But evening was coming. Soon, he could not see the words in his book. A few yards away, a nightingale in a bush began to sing its song.

Then Fitzpiers saw someone walking slowly through the woods. It was Grace! She came from behind a tree and she saw Fitzpiers sitting by the fire. For a moment, she did not recognize him. She screamed with fright.

Fitzpiers stood up quickly.

'I am sorry, Miss Melbury. I frightened you,' he said. He held her arm. 'But why have you come back?' he asked.

'I left my purse here,' Grace replied. 'There is not much money in it. But the purse was a present from a friend. I don't want to lose it.'

'Then we will find it,' Fitzpiers said. 'Is this friend a man? Is he an admirer, perhaps?'

'He did admire me,' Grace replied. 'But I do not meet

42

He looked at Grace and at the woods around him.

him any more.'

'Miss Melbury, I think that this man was in love with you. I think that you sent him away,' Fitzpiers said.

'Well, that is the truth,' Grace replied. 'I sent him away. But I pity him. I like him, too.'

'But pity is not love,' Fitzpiers said. 'I am interested in love, Miss Melbury. Perhaps, one day —?'

Grace did not answer him. Soon, Fitzpiers found the purse and gave it to Grace. She thanked him and walked quietly away.

7

Midsummer's Eve

It was Midsummer's Eve – the day before the longest day of the year. In the woodland, the leaves were thick and green on the trees. And by this time, Edred Fitzpiers was sure that he was in love with Grace.

By eleven o'clock that night, the moon was shining brightly. From his garden, Fitzpiers could see the excited village girls walking together towards the woods.

'Where are you going?' he called out. One of them – a pretty dark-haired girl called Suke Damson – answered him.

'We always go into the woods on Midsummer's Eve to find out who our husbands will be,' she said with a laugh. 'Every one of us wants to know who she is going to marry!'

Fitzpiers smiled. He waited for a few minutes and then he followed the girls.

The village girls, laughing and talking, were walking along a little path towards the darkest part of the woods. Fitzpiers was not the only person who was watching them.

Marty South and Grace Melbury were there. All the young village men were there too. Giles Winterbourne was standing near a big old oak tree.

Suke Damson saw Grace and called out to her.

'Why don't you come with us?' she said. 'We are going to scatter some seeds and say some magic words. Then, when the bell of the church clock rings twelve times, we'll all run back this way – into our lovers' arms!'

So Grace followed the village girls. Giles Winterbourne and Edred Fitzpiers had both heard Suke's words. They stood close to the path. Each man hoped that Grace would see him first.

Everything was quiet. Then the bell of the church clock rang twelve times. Midnight! The excited girls began to scream. Then they turned and ran back through the tall, dark trees.

Grace was one of the first girls to reach the place where the men were waiting. Fitzpiers stepped out in front of Giles Winterbourne and caught Grace in his arms.

She cried out in surprise.

'Now you are in my arms, dearest!' Fitzpiers said. 'I am going to keep you here for the rest of your life!'

When he heard these words, Giles turned and walked quickly away. Grace did not see him. She stood very still.

'Doctor Fitzpiers, please let me go,' she said.

Fitzpiers laughed, but kept his arms around the girl.

After a few moments, she pushed him away and she walked sadly home. But Fitzpiers was happy. He had held Grace in his arms. One day she would be his.

But as soon as Grace had gone, another girl ran past him.

'You can kiss me if you can catch me, Tim Tangs!' she called out. It was the dark-haired Suke Damson, the girl who had spoken to the doctor earlier. She laughed as she ran, and Fitzpiers ran after her. The girl knew the woodlands well and Fitzpiers could not catch her there. But then she ran out of the woods, into a hayfield[30]. In a moment, Suke had covered herself with dry hay.

Fitzpiers ran into the field and then he stood still for a moment in the bright moonlight. Suddenly, he heard Suke laughing quietly and he quickly found her.

'Doctor Fitzpiers! I thought that you were my lover, Tim Tangs!' Suke said, laughing again.

'Are you disappointed?' Fitzpiers asked. As he spoke, he kissed her. 'Are you?' he repeated.

'No,' Suke answered softly and the doctor kissed her again. Suke looked very beautiful in the moonlight. The two young people were alone. Little Hintock was two miles away. They did not return until daylight.

———

A week had passed since Midsummer's Eve. The weather was fine and bright. Fitzpiers thought of nothing but Grace Melbury. He wanted to marry her very much. Grace was only a village girl, but he did not care. He would marry her and perhaps he would stay in Little Hintock.

One morning, while he was thinking about Grace, Fitzpiers had a visitor – Grace's father.

'I have come to ask you about my daughter,' Mr Melbury began. Fitzpiers looked at him in surprise.

'Yes, I am thinking of sending her to stay by the sea,' Grace's father went on. 'She has a cough[31] and I am worried about her. I want you to tell me the best place for her to stay.'

'The best place for your daughter is here in Little Hintock,' Fitzpiers replied. 'She is not ill. But I do want to speak to you about her, Mr Melbury. I would like to know your daughter better.'

Mr Melbury was very surprised.

'You would like to know her better?' he repeated. 'Do you want to marry her, then?'

Fitzpiers could not catch her there. But then she ran out of the woods, into a hayfield.

'Yes, I do,' Fitzpiers answered.

'Well, if Grace agrees, I won't object to your plan,' Melbury said. 'You are a gentleman and I have educated Grace to be a lady. Sir, I am very pleased about this. You come from a good family. Tell Grace that you want to marry her. I am sure that she will be as happy about your plan as I am.'

The timber-merchant hurried home to speak to his wife.

'Lucy, I have some good news!' he said. 'A gentleman wishes to marry Grace. Where is she? I must speak to her!'

'She is upstairs in her bedroom. But who is the gentleman?' Mrs Melbury asked in surprise.

'Grace! Come down here at once!' her father called.

'What is it, Father?' Grace asked when she had come downstairs.

'You have only been home from school for six months. And already that fine young doctor is in love with you. He wants to know you better!'

'You mean that he wants to marry me?' Grace asked.

'Yes, of course,' Mr Melbury replied. 'Isn't that the reason why I have given you a good education? I'm sure that the doctor will take you away from Little Hintock. You will soon be living in good society.'

'I do not know what to say,' Grace replied. 'I know that the doctor is very clever. But I have not forgotten Giles —'

'Giles has ended his engagement to you,' Mr Melbury said quickly. 'Don't think about him any more. He doesn't have a house now. You deserve a better man. Doctor Fitzpiers' family used to own all the land around the village of Oakbury Fitzpiers.'

Suddenly, Mr Melbury looked at his daughter's face. Then he spoke more kindly.

'Giles is a good friend of mine, but he's not a gentleman, Grace,' he said. 'He will always be a woodlander. I want

48

somebody better for you. Don't you understand?'

Soon after this, Fitzpiers visited the Melburys' house. He did not feel at ease there. But before he left, he kissed Grace. And soon Grace believed that she was in love with the doctor.

The summer weeks went by. Fitzpiers talked to Grace about their future life together. The young woman admired him more and more. Her father was pleased. He looked forward to the time when his daughter would be the doctor's wife.

———

One evening, Grace Melbury and Edred Fitzpiers were returning to the village. They had been walking in the woods. They passed Hintock House, which was still closed up and empty.

'That is the kind of house that you should live in,' Fitzpiers said. 'But we will not live anywhere near Little Hintock. One day, I will probably buy a practice[32] in Budmouth. Budmouth is only twenty miles away, Grace dear. So I want you to agree to a plan which I have been thinking about.'

'What is that?' Grace asked.

'It is a plan about our wedding. I do not want us to get married here, in Hintock church,' Fitzpiers said. 'I do not want the villagers to look at us and talk about us.'

'Where shall we get married then? At a church in Budmouth?' Grace asked. She was surprised.

'Well, we shall get married in Budmouth, dear, but not in a church,' Fitzpiers replied. 'A quiet registry office[33] would be a much better place. So let us get married in a registry office in Budmouth, in one month's time.'

'No! I want to be married in the village church here, with my friends around me,' Grace said.

'Grace, listen to me!' Fitzpiers said. 'I do not want people to say, "Why is a clever doctor marrying a village girl?" No one in Budmouth will know about your life here in Little Hintock. Everyone there will think that I have married a lady. People will respect us more.'

'We can get married in a church in Budmouth,' Grace said.

'No, no,' Fitzpiers replied. 'A registry office will be better. Your father agrees with me. Why will you not agree? There is no need to marry in a church.'

Grace sighed.

'I do not like to hear you say that, Edred,' she said sadly. 'But I suppose that I must agree to your plan.'

When Grace was alone that night, she felt very unhappy. She knew that Fitzpiers was clever, but she did not like some of his ideas. And she was going to marry him in one month!

8

Marriage

That night, Grace could not sleep. She was worried. The next morning, she got up very early and she looked out of her bedroom window. Everything was quiet. She looked at the houses and cottages, at the woods and orchards. Then she looked at the house on the little hill where Edred Fitzpiers lived.

At that moment, the front door of the doctor's house opened and a woman came out. She was wearing a nightdress and a long grey cloak. The woman turned for a moment to look at the man who was standing inside the house. Then she hurried away.

Grace had seen the woman clearly. It was Suke Damson!

Grace stayed in her room for nearly three hours. She did not know what to do or what to think. Then she heard her parents talking downstairs. She got dressed and she went out into the garden to speak to her father.

'Good morning, my dear,' Mr Melbury said cheerfully. 'You must be a happy girl, Grace. In one month's time, you will be married!'

'I have been thinking about that, Father,' Grace said sadly. 'I do not wish to marry Doctor Fitzpiers.'

'You don't wish to marry Fitzpiers!' Mr Melbury said. He was surprised. And suddenly, he was worried.

'I do not wish to marry anyone, Father,' Grace went on. 'But if *you* want me to marry, I will marry Giles Winterbourne.'

Now Mr Melbury was very angry.

'Oh, you cruel, ungrateful girl!' he said. 'You have been meeting Giles Winterbourne secretly, haven't you?'

'No, father, but I saw Doctor Fitzpiers with a woman this morning. I —'

'Oh, you are jealous, you silly girl,' Mr Melbury said. Then he laughed. 'Look, I can see Fitzpiers in his garden now. I'll bring him here. He'll soon make things right between you.'

The timber-merchant called to the doctor, who started to walk towards the Melburys' house. Grace did not want to see Fitzpiers and she began to walk along the lane towards the woods. But Fitzpiers hurried after her.

'My darling, what is wrong?' he said. 'Let me kiss you and everything will be right again!'

Grace turned her head away.

'Doctor Fitzpiers, I looked out of my window a few hours ago. I cannot tell you what I saw. I am sure that you understand me.'

Fitzpiers understood at once.

'A girl from the village came to me very early this morning,' he explained. 'She had a terrible toothache. She begged me to

51

pull out the bad tooth, and I did. Then she went away. That is what you saw, my dear Grace.'

Grace believed Fitzpiers' story. In a moment, she was happy again. Fitzpiers kissed her and this time, she did not turn away. The two young people walked back towards the Melburys' garden.

'You are friends again, I see,' said Mr Melbury, who had been watching them.

'Oh, yes,' Fitzpiers said, and Grace smiled. She thought for a moment.

'I *will* marry Edred, but we must get married in a church,' she said.

'Then we *will* get married in a church,' Fitzpiers said quickly. 'I want to please you, Grace.'

From that moment, Fitzpiers was very careful. He saw Grace every day and did his best to make her happy.

In Little Hintock, the woodlanders' lives went on as usual – all except for Giles Winterbourne's. Now that Giles had no house, he had sold his furniture and he had left the village. People said that he would return in the autumn when the cider-making season began. But long before that, Fitzpiers and Grace had married. They married in August, and they went away on their honeymoon.

It was October when Doctor and Mrs Fitzpiers returned to Little Hintock. On the day before their return to the village, they stayed for a night at the 'Earl of Wessex', the best hotel in Sherton Abbas.

The next morning, Grace was sitting alone by the window of their room, looking down at the hotel yard. In the yard, men were bringing apples to a cider-press. As the fruit was pressed, the sweet juice ran out and it was collected in wooden buckets. Hundreds of baskets of apples were carried into the yard.

The air was full of the sweet smell of the ripe fruit.

The cider-press belonged to Giles Winterbourne. And soon, the young man himself was standing in the yard. His hair and his clothes were covered with tiny pieces of apple.

Grace remembered the time when she and Giles had been engaged. Then she smiled and she looked at the beautiful new rings on her white hands.

'I could not have married Giles,' she said to herself. 'The life of a travelling cider-maker's wife would have been too hard for me.'

But Grace was happy to see her old friend. She leant from the window and she called to Giles.

'Mr Winterbourne! Have you forgotten me?'

Giles looked up and then he walked slowly towards the window.

'Why are you speaking to me?' he said. 'I'm a working man. And you are a lady now, Mrs Fitzpiers. We can no longer be friends.'

'Giles – I am sorry,' Grace said. 'I did not want to hurt you.'

Giles smiled. He could not be angry with Grace for long. He was happy to see her again. Giles asked her about her journey and Grace was happy to talk about it. At the end of their conversation, Giles returned to his work and Grace felt very sad. She felt pity for the friend who she had known all her life. She shut the window quietly.

At that moment, her husband came into the room.

'I have been talking to Mr Winterbourne,' Grace said.

'You have nothing to talk to him about,' Fitzpiers said quickly. 'Your education has made you a lady. And you are married to a doctor. You should not speak to a cider-maker. You are better than Winterbourne now.'

'I do not *feel* better than him,' Grace replied. 'I am sorry, but you will have to accept that.'

'You are a lady now, Mrs Fitzpiers. We can no longer be friends.'

For a moment, Fitzpiers did not reply. Then he smiled suddenly. 'I will try to accept it,' he said.

That afternoon, the two young people began their journey to Little Hintock.

Grace was very happy to be returning to her beloved woodland. But Edred Fitzpiers was not looking forward to living in the Melburys' house.

'Has this marriage been a mistake?' he asked himself. 'Little Hintock is not the right place for me! I know that!'

George and Lucy Melbury had invited several of their village friends to a meal that evening. Everyone sat at the table. Everyone laughed and talked. Everyone except Fitzpiers. He did not laugh and he did not talk.

Later that night, the young doctor spoke to his wife.

'I am sure that the visitors enjoyed themselves tonight, Grace,' he said. 'But that must be the last time we meet these villagers. We must stay in our own rooms in future. We are better than these villagers. We cannot mix with them now.'

'Very well, dear,' Grace replied.

The next day, Fitzpiers began his work as a doctor again. But the villagers no longer respected him. He had married the timber-merchant's daughter. The villagers thought that he had become a woodlander like themselves.

At the end of two weeks, Fitzpiers had made a decision. Late one evening, he told Grace about it.

'I have heard about a practice in Budmouth, Grace,' he said. 'I want to buy it. It will cost about eight hundred pounds. I want your father to lend me some of the money. Then we can leave Little Hintock for ever.'

At that moment, there was a knock at the door. It was a servant from Hintock House. He had a message from Mrs Charmond. She had had an accident in her carriage. She wanted the doctor to visit her at once.

Fitzpiers got ready quickly.

'I shall be asleep when you come back,' Grace said to her husband. 'Good night, Edred.'

'Good night,' Fitzpiers said as he hurried from the room. It was the first time that he had left his wife without kissing her.

9

Two Friends Meet Again

Fitzpiers soon arrived at Hintock House, and a servant took him into a pleasant sitting-room. Mrs Charmond was sitting on a couch. Her beautiful thick hair was shiny in the light of a small lamp. She looked up at the handsome young doctor and smiled.

Fitzpiers looked into her eyes. For a moment, he could not speak. Then he asked her a few questions about her accident. She told him that she had a pain in her shoulder and he examined it carefully. He could find nothing wrong.

'Your shoulder is not badly injured, but you must rest for a while,' he said.

'Oh,' she said. 'But my arm is hurting me. Please put a bandage on it for me.'

Fitzpiers wrapped a bandage round Mrs Charmond's arm. She smiled at him.

'We have met before, Doctor Fitzpiers,' she said. 'Do you not remember? You were studying in Germany. I was there with my mother. We all stayed in the same hotel.'

'Yes! You were the young woman with the beautiful hair,' Fitzpiers said slowly. 'I saw you and I fell in love with you immediately. We only spoke once, and you told me your name – Felice. I remember that! The next day, you had left

56

'I saw you and I fell in love with you immediately.'

the hotel. I did not forget you for days and days!'

'Only for days and days?' Mrs Charmond repeated, laughing. 'Ah! Men's hearts are always changing!'

'But now we have met again,' Fitzpiers said. 'Now our friendship can grow. Perhaps it will last for ever!'

'I hope that you are right,' Mrs Charmond replied. 'Please come here again tomorrow.'

Fitzpiers left Hintock House. He did not know what to think. He had once been in love with Felice Charmond. Was he going to fall in love with her again?

Grace was not asleep when he returned.

'Edred, is Mrs Charmond seriously injured?' Grace asked.

'Injured? No! Well – yes! I must visit her again tomorrow.'

———

Fitzpiers went back to Hintock House the next day, and the next day, and the next. Hour after hour, Felice Charmond and Edred Fitzpiers were alone together.

On the fourth day, Felice found out that Fitzpiers was planning to leave Little Hintock and live in Budmouth.

'Of course, I understand your reasons!' Felice Charmond exclaimed. 'Who wants to live in Little Hintock? I know that you hate the place. I am sure that you would not stay here for me!'

Later, while he was on his way home, Fitzpiers made another decision. He decided to stay in Little Hintock. That evening, he told Grace about his new plan. She was surprised. She did not think that her husband was happy in the village.

———

Doctor Fitzpiers did not go back to Hintock House for two or three days. When he did return, Felice Charmond was not kind to him.

'Oh, how I hate my life!' she said.

'Why? What is wrong, Felice?' Fitzpiers asked.

58

'I have decided that you must not come here again,' Mrs Charmond replied. 'That will be best for both of us.'

'But why? What do you mean?' Fitzpiers asked.

'Well, I cannot stay here, alone in this house,' she replied. 'The villagers will start to talk about us. I am going to stay with a relation, at Middleton Abbey. When are you and your pretty young wife going to live in Budmouth?'

'We are not going to live in Budmouth,' Fitzpiers replied.

'Oh, that is *my* fault!' Felice Charmond said. 'Now I have spoilt your career! Well, I shall be more than ten miles away for a month or two.'

'May I write to you?' Fitzpiers asked.

'No, no. That would not be right,' Mrs Charmond replied.

'Very well. Goodbye,' Fitzpiers said. In a moment, he had gone.

––––––

That evening, Felice Charmond asked her maid about Fitzpiers' marriage to Grace.

'Miss Melbury was engaged to another man before the doctor came here,' the maid said.

'Then why did she not marry him?' Mrs Charmond asked.

'Well, the man was Mr Winterbourne. He lost the lease on his house. Your lawyer wouldn't extend the lease, although he extended Marty South's. Then, because Mr Winterbourne had no house, he couldn't get married.'

Mrs Charmond did not say any more to the maid.

'My lawyer treated Mr Winterbourne badly,' she thought. 'Because of that, Grace Melbury married the man that I love. Life is cruel! How unhappy I am!'

A day or two later, she left Hintock House and she went to Middleton Abbey.

––––––

Doctor Fitzpiers did not always drive in his gig when he visited his patients. He often rode Grace's grey horse,

Darling, instead.

One day, when he had been out on Darling, Fitzpiers came home very late. The doctor and the horse were both very tired.

Grace met her husband at the stable and held his arm as he walked into the house. Suddenly, a ticket fell out of Fitzpiers' pocket. Grace picked it up and looked at it. It was a toll ticket[34] for the Middleton Gate turnpike.

The next day, Grace found out that Mrs Charmond was staying at Middleton Abbey. And a few days later, she learnt that Fitzpiers had travelled on the Middleton road again.

Grace was sure that her husband was visiting Mrs Charmond. But she did not feel angry or jealous. She did not care any more.

The next time he went out, Grace watched her husband carefully. She hid in the trees beside the lane and watched him ride out of the village. It was already late afternoon, but Fitzpiers turned in the direction of Middleton Abbey. Because Darling was a grey horse, Grace could see it clearly against the green of the trees. She watched the horse and its rider for several minutes. At last, she turned and walked slowly into the woods herself.

On her way through the woods, Grace met Giles Winterbourne. The young woodlander looked very handsome and his clothes had the rich, sweet smell of ripe apples. Grace stopped to talk to him. Suddenly she began to feel like a country girl again – a country girl who had once been in love with this young man.

The sun was beginning to set and the western sky shone with red and orange light. But Grace's face was sad. She had been married for only a few months, and her husband had already started meeting another woman.

Giles seemed to understand her sadness. There was a flower pinned on Grace's dress. The young man reached out his hand and touched the flower.

'Giles, you must not do that!' Grace said. 'I am not your wife!'

'I'm sorry, Mrs Fitzpiers,' Giles replied angrily. 'I forgot who you are for a moment. And I forgot who I am! I forgot that you are a lady now and I am only a woodlander. But I saw somebody – a gentleman – do the same thing at Middleton Abbey, when I was there recently. And the lady wasn't *his* wife.'

'Who was the – gentleman?' Grace asked quietly.

'Please don't ask me,' Giles replied.

'It was my husband,' Grace said sadly. 'And the woman was Mrs Charmond. I know that they meet each other and you know it too. But I do not want to talk about it. And please do not say anything about it to my father! I am going home now, Giles.'

In a few minutes, Grace came to a wide path with hazel bushes on either side. Suke Damson was standing there, picking the ripe nuts from one of the bushes. She was cracking the nuts open with her strong teeth.

'Be careful, Suke, or you will get a toothache again,' Grace called to the girl.

'Oh, I've never had a toothache in all my life,' Suke replied. 'And I still have all my teeth. Look!' She pointed at her open mouth.

'Then you are a lucky girl, Suke,' Grace said. She walked on through the wood.

'So Edred lied about Suke's tooth too,' Grace thought. 'I have married a cruel, weak man! But I don't care any more. If he cannot love only me, I will not love him!'

———

Fitzpiers had not returned home when Grace went to bed that night. And in the morning, she was still alone. She got dressed quickly and went downstairs. She told her father that Fitzpiers had not come back.

'Then we must go and look for him,' Mr Melbury said.

As they walked past the stable, Grace looked inside. She saw her grey horse in there. And she saw Fitzpiers sitting on the horse's back! He was asleep!

Grace went up to her husband and touched his hand. He opened his eyes at once.

'Ah, Felice —! Oh, it's you, Grace. I could not see you in the darkness,' Fitzpiers said quickly.

Mr Melbury was standing by the stable door. He heard Fitzpiers' words. He knew that something was very wrong.

'Why did I let Grace marry that man?' Mr Melbury asked himself. 'And why is Mrs Felice Charmond trying to steal my daughter's husband? I must find out more about that lady.'

10

Mrs Charmond

Winter had come to the woodlands again. This winter, Mrs Charmond had not gone abroad. She had returned from Middleton Abbey and she was living at Hintock House again.

One December morning, Edred Fitzpiers stood looking out of his bedroom window.

'How boring my life is!' he said aloud. 'Why am I living in this village? Because I fell in love with a village girl! What a fool I was!'

He turned and looked at the bed. Was Grace asleep? Had she heard him? Fitzpiers did not know and he did not care. He was very unhappy.

Grace was unhappy too. She did not love her husband any

more, she loved Giles Winterbourne. She had pitied Giles, and now her pity for him had turned into love.

George Melbury knew that his daughter was unhappy. Later that morning, he decided to talk to her.

'You are not happy with your husband, Grace,' he said. 'We both know who has made you unhappy.'

'Well, Father, what can I do about it?' Grace asked sadly.

'Go to Mrs Charmond. Talk to her,' Mr Melbury said. 'She is a woman too. She was your friend once. Tell her what you know. You could stop her friendship with your husband.'

'No! I could never talk to her about Edred,' Grace said. 'And she and my husband can do what they like. I do not care.'

'You *must* care, Grace!' her father replied. 'You have been well educated. You are used to good society. Your marriage is important.'

'I hate society. I hate my education!' Grace said. 'And I hate my marriage. I wish that I worked in the woods like Marty South. Then I could marry —'

Grace, was almost crying now. She ran from the room.

'I must do something to help Grace,' Mr Melbury said to himself. 'But what *can* I do?'

As winter passed into spring, all the woodlanders knew that something was wrong with Grace Melbury's marriage. Stories about Fitzpiers and Mrs Charmond were told by one villager to another.

At last, George Melbury decided to talk to Giles Winterbourne about Grace's trouble. He had not seen Giles for a long time. But he knew that the young man was living in a little cottage in the woods. Giles had been very ill that winter, but Melbury did not know this. Giles had told no one about his illness.

One day, when Edred Fitzpiers was away visiting London, George Melbury went into the woods to look for his young friend. He found Giles working in a hazel plantation. In the middle of the plantation, the smoke from a little fire was rising in the damp air. Giles was working near the fire. He had cut down some young trees and he was using the wood to make hurdles for fences.

Mr Melbury sighed. 'Ah, Giles, you should have been my business partner,' he said. 'And you should have been my son-in-law too.'

Giles stopped working.

'Is there trouble at your house, sir?' he asked.

'Yes, there is bad trouble,' Mr Melbury replied. 'I made a mistake about that doctor. *You* should have married my daughter. I know that now.'

'But I'm not an educated man,' Giles said. 'I couldn't give Grace the things that she needs.'

'Grace hates education now!' Mr Melbury said. 'She wants to be like Marty South. She wants to work in the woods! Grace loved you once, Giles. I think that she *still* loves you.'

Giles did not answer, but the timber-merchant's words made him happy. He was still in love with Grace.

'I might talk to Mrs Charmond about this trouble,' Melbury went on. 'But I'm not sure if that will help. Do you know anything about that woman?'

'She was an actress before she got married,' Giles said. 'Her husband was much older than her. She has had many lovers.'

Mr Melbury frowned.

'But people say that she is sometimes kind,' Giles added. 'Perhaps she is not really a bad person.'

'Then I *will* talk to her,' Melbury replied.

Melbury had made his decision. He left Giles and he walked quickly home.

———

At nine o'clock the next morning, Mr Melbury put on his best clothes and he walked to Hintock House. When he arrived, Mrs Charmond was still in her bed. He had to wait for two hours before he could speak to her.

At last, Mrs Charmond came into the room where the timber-merchant was waiting.

'Have you come about my beech trees, Mr Melbury?' she asked.

'No, I haven't come about trees,' Mr Melbury replied. 'I have come about my daughter, Grace. She is very unhappy. You are making her unhappy, Mrs Charmond. I gave her a good education and she has married a gentleman. But this gentleman came here and met you, and then the trouble started. Please stop meeting my son-in-law, Mrs Charmond. Then perhaps he will be happy with my daughter again.'

Mrs Charmond went pale.

'What do you mean?' she exclaimed. 'What are people saying about me?'

'You must have heard about the stories that the villagers are telling,' the timber-merchant said. 'You were once my daughter's friend. Have you forgotten that?'

'Yes, no — oh, please go away, Mr Melbury!' Mrs Charmond said.

'Yes, I will leave you to think about this,' Mr Melbury said quietly.

The timber-merchant left the house. He was too upset to go home. He started to walk towards Sherton Abbas.

When she was alone, Felice Charmond began to cry. She stood up and walked round the room. She did not know what to do. She could not talk to her lover – he was in London. She could not stay in the house. She put on a thick coat and she was soon walking towards the woods.

———

In the afternoon, Grace started to ask herself where her father had gone. And soon, she guessed that he had gone to Hintock House. She decided to meet him. She left the house at about three o'clock and she started to walk along the path through the woods.

The first person that she saw was Giles. He was working in the hazel plantation. Marty South was working nearby.

'I am looking for my father,' Grace said to Giles. 'I am sure that he went to Hintock House this morning.'

'Yes, I think that you're right,' Giles replied. 'And I know the reason for his visit, Grace. I spoke to him yesterday. He was very worried. We talked about Mrs Charmond.'

'Oh, I am so glad that you talked to Father! You are friends with him again,' Grace said.

Because the two young people were looking at each other, they had not seen Mrs Charmond walk into the plantation. But at that moment, she was talking quietly to Marty South.

'Who is the young lady who is talking to the woodlander?' she asked Marty. 'And who is he?'

'The lady is Mrs Fitzpiers,' Marty said. 'She is talking to Mr Winterbourne.' Suddenly, Marty blushed.

'Mr Winterbourne. Ah, yes. Are you engaged to him?' Mrs Charmond asked quietly.

'No, I'm not engaged to Mr Winterbourne,' Marty replied. 'But *she* was once.'

Mrs Charmond thought for a moment and then she walked towards Giles and Grace. Giles saw her coming.

'Mrs Charmond wants to talk to you,' he said to Grace. 'She doesn't like me. I'll leave you alone with her.'

Mrs Charmond held out her hand to Grace, but Grace turned away.

'Mrs Fitzpiers, I would like to talk to you,' Felice Charmond said. 'Will you walk with me, please?'

The two women walked on into the woods. For a while, neither of them spoke.

'I have seen your father,' Mrs Charmond said at last. 'He spoke to me about Doctor Fitzpiers – your husband.' She stopped speaking. She could not say anything more.

Grace looked at the older woman's face.

'Ah, I understand now,' Grace said. 'I thought that you were just playing a game with my husband. But you love him! I can see that now. Oh, I do not hate you, I pity you. Edred is playing a game with you. He will make you very unhappy!'

'No, no, you are very cruel to say that,' Mrs Charmond said. 'I was lonely. I wanted someone to talk to. That is all.'

'You can love him – I do not care,' Grace replied. 'You will never win his love. He gets bored with people very quickly. He will get bored with *you* very soon.'

'That is nonsense,' Felice Charmond replied. She was very angry now and wanted to hurt Grace. 'You do not know me and you do not know Edred, you foolish child,' she went on. 'Now you must know the truth. Shall I tell you the truth about your husband and me?'

There was no need for the older woman to say any more.

'So, my husband is your lover,' said Grace. 'You are both cruel, unhappy people. But I no longer care. I will keep your secret. See him as often as you like. Goodbye.'

———

Edred Fitzpiers was staying in London for a week. Grace wanted to get away from Little Hintock for a few days. She decided to visit one of her friends in Shottsford Forum.

Grace was still at her friend's house when Fitzpiers returned to Little Hintock, late one afternoon. He was angry because his wife was not at home. And he was angry because he had heard some news. Mrs Charmond was going abroad again soon.

'I have to see Felice,' Fitzpiers said to himself. He got onto Grace's horse and rode towards Hintock House.

As he passed Marty South's cottage, Marty ran towards the doctor.

'Shall I tell you the truth about your husband and me?'

'This is for you,' she said to Fitzpiers. She gave him a letter. The doctor took the letter and put it in his pocket. Then he rode on. He forgot about the letter almost at once.

If he had opened it, Fitzpiers would have read this:

> *Doctor Fitzpiers*
> *Mrs Charmond has deceived you. You love her beautiful hair. But it is not all her own hair. Mrs Charmond wears a hair-piece that was made from my hair.*
> *Can you love her now?*
>
> *Marty South*

Fitzpiers rode on to Hintock House. He got off the grey horse and he tied its reins[35] to a tree at the side of the house. Then he walked to the front door.

At the same time, George Melbury was returning from a visit to Shottsford Forum. He had visited Grace there. She had a cold and she wanted to come home to Little Hintock. But she felt ill and she did not want to ride in the gig. So her father had hired a comfortable carriage and she was going to travel home in that.

Mr Melbury was very angry when he discovered that Fitzpiers had returned home and then had gone immediately to Hintock House.

'I shall ride there and bring him back,' Mr Melbury told his wife. 'Grace will be home in two hours' time. And her husband must be here when she arrives!'

It was nearly dark by now, but when Mr Melbury arrived at Hintock House, he could see the grey horse, Darling, tied to the tree. He tied his own horse to the tree too, and he walked quickly towards the front door.

The door was open. Mr Melbury walked quietly into the house, listening carefully. Then he heard some sounds in the sitting-room. He pushed open the door. As he entered the room, Felice Charmond and his son-in-law were going out of a door at the other end of the room. They were going into the garden. Mrs Charmond was holding the doctor's arm.

Mr Melbury followed them into the garden. He saw Fitzpiers and Mrs Charmond saying goodbye to each other at the end of the lawn. They kissed each other, then Mrs Charmond turned back towards the house. George Melbury waited a few moments and then he hurried after Fitzpiers.

When he reached the tree where the horses had been tied, Mr Melbury saw that Fitzpiers had gone. And he also saw that his own horse had gone. The grey horse was still there.

'Fitzpiers has taken the wrong horse!' Mr Melbury said to himself. 'My horse is difficult to ride. Fitzpiers will have an accident. I must ride after him.'

Mr Melbury got onto Darling and he rode through the wood. He soon saw his own horse. But the horse had no rider. As he got nearer, the horse saw him and it ran away. Then Mr Melbury saw Fitzpiers lying on the ground. The timber-merchant's horse had thrown the doctor off.

Mr Melbury helped his son-in-law to sit up. He gave the young man some brandy from a silver bottle which he carried in his pocket. Then he pushed Fitzpiers onto Darling and got onto the horse behind him. He held the doctor with one hand and the horse's reins with the other. He started to ride back towards his house.

Fitzpiers had not eaten for many hours. The brandy quickly made him drunk. He did not recognize his father-in-law and he began to talk very foolishly.

'I wish that I lived in London,' he said. 'I married a silly country girl, and now I have to live in an awful country village. Only one person here understands me – the person I should have married! If only I had met her a few months earlier! Now I shall never be happy. I shall never be free, unless —'

George Melbury could not listen to any more of this.

'You wicked young man!' he shouted. 'Stop saying these things to me! You've used my money and you live in my house. And now you are saying wicked things about my daughter!'

As he spoke, Mr Melbury angrily pushed Fitzpiers off the horse. The doctor hit his head on the trunk of a tree. But before Mr Melbury could stop and help him, Fitzpiers got up. He walked away quickly into the woods.

'Well, he isn't hurt,' Melbury said to himself. He rode on towards his house. He soon found his own horse, and walking slowly, he took the two animals back to the stable.

———

Somebody else had seen Fitzpiers in the wood. Before Mr Melbury came, a boy from the village had seen the doctor riding the timber-merchant's horse. Fitzpiers had been riding the difficult horse too fast, and the horse had thrown him off. The boy had not tried to help the doctor. He had run back to the village and he had told some of the villagers that Fitzpiers was dying! Soon, most people in the village had heard this news.

When Grace returned home, her mother told her the boy's news. Grace went up to her bedroom, to get the bed ready for the dying man.

As she came out of the bedroom, she heard someone crying in the hall below. She looked down the stairs. Suke Damson was standing in the hall, with tears running down her face. When she saw Grace, she hurried up the stairs towards her.

'Oh, Mrs Fitzpiers, I had to come,' Suke said. 'You must let me see Edred. Is he badly injured? Is he dead? Please tell me!'

Before Grace could answer, she saw Felice Charmond come into the hall.

'What is wrong?' Mrs Charmond said. 'Is Edred alive or is he dead? You must tell me, Grace!'

Grace said nothing, but Suke pointed to the bedroom door.

'He's in there! He's dying!' she said.

'He is *not* in there,' Grace said coldly. 'You can go in and look, if you want to. I do not care. You have both seen my husband in bedrooms before. But he is not in that bedroom now!'

At that moment, Grace heard her father's voice. She ran down the stairs.

'Is Edred badly injured?' she asked Mr Melbury. 'Do *you* know anything about this?'

'He isn't hurt at all,' Mr Melbury replied. 'He took my horse and it threw him off. Later, he fell off his own horse. But he got up and walked away. I don't know where he is now.'

'Why did you not look for him?' Grace asked.

'Well, we had an argument,' her father replied. 'Perhaps he won't come back here tonight. I hope that he doesn't! Why do you care where he is?'

'He *is* my husband,' Grace said. 'First, you wanted him to marry me, Father. Now you want him to leave me. Well, I will wait for him here.'

Fitzpiers' two lovers went quietly away. Later, Mr Melbury went to bed. After that, Grace waited alone. But her husband did not return.

11

Bad News

Felice Charmond was sitting alone in Hintock House. It was very late in the evening.

'I must leave this place,' she said to herself. 'I must get away from Little Hintock and from Edred Fitzpiers!'

At that moment, she heard a noise. It came from outside the door which led to the garden. She got up quickly and opened the door. She looked into the pale, blood-stained face of the man who stood outside. Then she turned and led her lover into the room.

'Sit down, Edred. Drink some water,' she said. 'What has happened to you? Are you badly injured?'

'No, I'm not badly injured,' Fitzpiers said. 'But you must hide me, my dear Felice. Hide me until I can get away from Little Hintock. You are my only friend now!'

Felice took the doctor to an empty bedroom. She washed the blood from his face and gently helped him to lie on the bed.

'You'll be safe here,' she said. Then she left the room and shut the door.

———

A few days later, Grace received a letter. It had been posted in Budmouth.

> *Dear Grace,*
> *Your father hates me, so I can no longer live in his house. I am going far away from Little Hintock now. You will not see me in the village for a long time.*
> *Edred Fitzpiers*

She looked into pale, blood-stained face of the man who stood outside.

Fitzpiers was *not* in Budmouth. Felice Charmond had posted the letter for him there. Fitzpiers stayed secretly at Hintock House until early May. He then left secretly, late one night. Three days later, Mrs Charmond herself left Hintock House.

Later, in the summer, there was some news in the village. A traveller had seen Edred Fitzpiers and Felice Charmond together in a fashionable town in Germany.

―――

George Melbury was a very unhappy man. He had wanted Grace to marry Fitzpiers. Now Fitzpiers had left her. Could his daughter ever be happy again? Mr Melbury talked about his family's troubles with everyone that he met.

In 1857, a divorce law[36] had been passed in England. This law said that some people who were unhappily married would be able to get divorced. And one day in the summer of that year, Mr Melbury heard about the new law.

After that, he was sure that the law would help his daughter. Fitzpiers had had a lover after his wedding and now he had left Grace and was living with his lover. Grace would be able to get divorced from her husband.

Mr Melbury soon told Giles Winterbourne about the new law.

'Everything will be all right, Giles my friend,' Melbury said. 'Grace will be able to divorce Fitzpiers and marry you!'

'Are you sure about that?' Giles asked.

'I'm not *sure* about it. But I'm going to London tomorrow, to speak to a good lawyer,' Mr Melbury replied. 'You and Grace will not have to wait for long.'

―――

Mr Melbury had been away for a week. One morning, Grace and Giles met in the woods.

'My dear Grace, you are prettier than ever,' Giles said. Grace smiled and Giles held her hand.

'You should not hold my hand yet, Giles,' Grace said. 'I am still married to Edred, although my father thinks that I will be able to get divorced. But you must wait till then.'

'Yes, Grace. I'll wait,' Giles said quietly.

'I am sure that my father will send good news in his next letter,' Grace said. 'I know that he wants me to marry you. But for the moment, we must only be friends.'

'Then we will walk together as friends,' Giles said.

Giles held Grace's arm, and they walked on towards the lane. Then Grace stopped and looked at the young man by her side.

'Oh, Giles,' Grace said. 'I will be free very soon. And I do love you. Please kiss me!'

Very gently, Giles held Grace in his arms and he kissed her.

'No, no!' shouted a voice behind them. They turned. Grace's father was running towards them.

'I'm sorry,' Mr Melbury said. 'I have bad news. You two can never be married and you mustn't walk together any more. Grace is still Fitzpiers' wife and she always will be. The new law is not for country people like us. Giles, you must stay away from Grace.'

Grace did not speak until she was alone with her father.

'I do not care what happens to me now,' she said sadly. 'But I love Giles. I will always love him.'

12

The Cottage in the Woods

For the next three months, life in the woodland went on as usual, but Grace and Giles did not meet each other. Then, one day, Grace received a letter from her husband.

Tuesday

Dear Grace,
I am now living alone in France. If you could forgive me, we could be together again. But I will not return to live in Little Hintock. I shall be travelling by boat to Budmouth in three days' time. Please meet me there on Saturday, Grace. We could get on the next boat to France, and we could live together here.

Edred

Grace showed the letter to her father.

'You must not go to live in France,' he said. 'If Fitzpiers comes back to live in England, you can go to him – he is your husband. But I will not let you live abroad.'

Grace did not want to live in France, and she did not want to meet her husband. But there was no address on Fitzpiers' letter, so she could not answer it. She stayed in Lower Hintock. She hoped that her husband would return to France when he did not find her in Budmouth.

But the next Monday, one of the villagers who had been in Budmouth brought news of Fitzpiers. The doctor had been seen at an inn in the town. He was on his way to Little Hintock. And he would arrive in less than an hour.

'Oh, I won't meet him, I won't!' Grace said angrily. She

ran upstairs to her bedroom. After some time, she heard the sound of a carriage in the lane. Then the carriage stopped for a moment and she clearly heard her husband's voice.

Grace made a decision. Quickly, she packed a few clothes into a bag. Then she wrote a note.

> *I have gone to visit one of my friends. I will be away for a week.*
>
> *Grace*

And, in a minute, she had left the house by the back door and was hurrying through the trees. She ran further and further into the woods. At last, she saw a light. It was coming from the window of a tiny cottage. There were leafy trees all round the cottage. It was a very secret place.

Grace went up to the cottage and looked through the window. The cottage had only one room. Inside, a small piece of meat was cooking over a fire. Giles Winterbourne was standing in front of the fire. This little cottage was his home now.

Giles' face was pale and very sad. When Grace knocked at the door, Giles walked very slowly towards it. But when he opened the door and saw Grace, he smiled.

Giles put his hands on Grace's arms. For a moment, the two young people stood looking at each other.

'Come in,' Giles said, very quietly.

'No, no, my dear friend,' Grace replied. 'I must not come in, but I want you to help me, Giles. I am going to get on a train at Sherton Abbas. Please come with me to the station. You are my only friend now.'

Grace could not say any more. Suddenly, she began to cry. Giles held her hand.

'What's happened?' he asked.

'My husband has come back to Little Hintock,' Grace

replied. 'Please help me to get away from him.'

'Yes! I'll come at once,' Giles said.

He picked up a lantern and the two young people began to walk through the woods. It was starting to rain, but the thick trees protected them. After a while, they came to an open place. They saw that it was now raining very heavily. Giles stopped.

'Grace,' he said. 'It's raining too hard. You can't go any further tonight.'

'But I cannot go back to —' Grace began.

'No, no. You must stay in my cottage tonight,' Giles told her. 'There is food there, and you will be warm and dry. Nobody will find you. I have another place nearby, where I can sleep.'

'Oh, Giles, I am so sorry,' Grace said. Then they turned and hurried back to the little cottage.

'Go inside,' Giles said. 'Lock the door. I'll come back in the morning.'

Giles went to a shelter which he had made in the woods nearby. The shelter was only a few hurdles fixed together. The rain came through the hurdles and Giles could not sleep. He had been ill already that autumn and he was weak. But the young man was happy, because Grace had come to him when she was in trouble.

In the morning, it was still raining. Giles knocked on the door of the cottage to wake Grace. She talked to him through the door for a few minutes, but she did not see him. She stayed inside the little cottage all that day. She thought that Giles was working somewhere in the woodlands.

In the evening, Giles came to the cottage again, and he spoke to Grace through the window. Now he had a bad fever, but he did not tell Grace about his illness. It was dark, so she could not see how ill he was.

'I think you should stay here for a few more days, Grace,'

Giles said. 'Then you must make a decision about your future.'

'You know that I love you, dear Giles,' Grace replied. 'I want to stay here with you for the rest of our lives. But the law says that I must go back to my husband.'

'I don't want you to go away,' Giles said.

'I know, I know,' Grace said. 'I want you to come inside and be with me now. But that would be wrong. We must do what is right.'

'Yes, Grace, I know that,' Giles replied. 'But stay here tonight. You will be safe here, and I will not be far away.'

Later that night, the wind became very strong. The rain continued to fall heavily. Grace was afraid, but she was dry and safe inside the cottage. She lay awake, thinking of Giles. She could not sleep. At last she got up and unlocked the door.

'Giles! Giles!' she called. 'Giles, do come inside. You must not stay out in this terrible wind and rain! Giles, I want you, my dearest. Come to me now. I do not care what anyone says about us. We *should* be in here, together!'

A weak voice answered her.

'Don't worry about me, Grace. Go inside and try to sleep. Good night, dear Grace, good night.'

Grace could do no more. She went inside and closed the door.

———

The rain continued all the next day. Giles did not come to the cottage. Night came again. It was twenty-four hours since Grace had seen Giles. She went to the door of the cottage and listened carefully.

She heard someone coughing. The sound was quite near. Grace picked up Giles' lantern and went out into the dark night. Twenty yards from the cottage, she found Giles in the shelter. She held up the light and she looked down at the woodlander. He was lying on a bed of wet hay. His clothes were very wet and his face was red with fever. Giles' eyes were open, but he did not recognize Grace.

'Oh, Giles! What have I done to you?' Grace said sadly. She knelt down, and kissed his hands and face.

'Oh, why didn't I think more about you?' the girl said. 'I have killed you, Giles! I have killed you! What shall I do now?'

Grace pulled Giles back to the little cottage. She gently washed his face and made him warm and dry. But Giles was very ill and he needed a doctor. And the nearest doctor was Grace's husband – Edred Fitzpiers.

When Giles fell asleep, Grace started to walk back to her father's house.

————

An hour later, Grace and Fitzpiers were standing together in the little cottage, looking down at Giles Winterbourne.

'Is he dying? Can you save him?' Grace asked. She held Giles' hand and gently touched his hair. In her thoughts, Fitzpiers was a doctor, not her husband.

'I cannot help him now,' Fitzpiers said. 'He is dying. He has been ill for a long time. I think that he has had typhoid[37] sometime in the last year. Now he is very weak.'

Grace knelt on the ground beside the bed. Giles was still asleep. He never woke again. In less than an hour, he was dead.

Grace cried bitterly. She held the dead man's hand and her tears fell on his face.

'He was *everything* to me!' she said.

Fitzpiers was very surprised at his wife's words. He was surprised, but he had to know the truth.

'Grace, I am your husband! I have come back to you,' he said angrily. 'I am living in your father's house again. But you have been here with this man. You said that he was *everything* to you. You must tell me, Grace. Were you this man's lover?'

'Yes,' Grace said. 'Yes! Yes!' It was a lie, but she wished that it was true.

Fitzpiers went very pale. Then he spoke very quietly.

'The man that you loved is dead,' he said. 'And the woman that I loved is dead too – Felice Charmond is dead. What are we going to do, Grace?'

Grace did not speak, but she kissed Giles' face again.

'Have you kissed him while he was ill?' Fitzpiers asked.

'Yes, I have kissed his lips – a thousand times!' Grace replied.

Fitzpiers took a little bottle from his pocket.

'Then you must drink this medicine, or *you* will soon be dead too,' he said.

Grace shook her head.

'I do not care. I want to die,' she said. 'I will not drink it!'

Fitzpiers put the little bottle on the table.

'I will leave it here,' he said. 'I am going to tell your father what has happened. Perhaps he will pay for your lover's funeral.'

Grace did not reply, and Fitzpiers quickly left the cottage.

A few minutes later, Marty South walked quietly into the little room. She looked down at Giles' face.

'Well, he has gone. He doesn't belong to either of us now, Mrs Fitzpiers,' Marty said. 'You can't bring him back with your beauty, and I can't bring him back with my love.'

Marty left the cottage, and soon, Mr and Mrs Melbury came to take Grace home.

Grace spoke to her worried parents gently.

'Listen! I did not tell my husband the truth,' she said. 'This dear good man gave me his home. We did not live here together. But I want to stay here now. I will not come home with you, because my husband is at the house.'

'Yes, I have kissed his lips – a thousand times!'

'We have spoken to him about that,' George Melbury said. 'Your husband will go away if you come home to us. Please come, Grace.'

Grace looked at Giles for the last time. Then she left the little cottage in the woods and started to walk home with her parents. On the way, they told her more about Mrs Charmond's death.

'She was not living with your husband when she died,' Mr Melbury said. 'They had an argument about her hair. Marty South sent Fitzpiers a letter about it.'

'Marty South?' Grace repeated in surprise.

'Yes. Mrs Charmond had bought Marty's hair and Mr Percomb had made a hair-piece from it,' Mr Melbury said. 'But Fitzpiers thought that Mrs Charmond's hair was all her own. She told him that it was. Then Marty told Fitzpiers about the hair-piece in a letter which she gave him in Little Hintock. But your husband didn't read the letter for a long time. He put it in his pocket and forgot about it. One day, in Germany, he found it. And when Fitzpiers read the letter, he was angry. He showed it to Mrs Charmond and then he left her. She tried to follow him, but she died soon afterwards.'

'She was my friend once,' Grace said sadly. 'She was an unhappy woman. She did not like growing older.'

They were now very near their home. Grace looked at her father.

'I will not live here again unless my husband leaves,' she said. 'Will you tell him that? I do not want to see him again.'

Mr Melbury nodded. Grace sat quietly in her parents' part of the house. An hour later, Fitzpiers went past the window with a bag in his hand. He looked at Grace for a moment and then he walked away up the lane.

13

Afterwards

A few days later, Grace became ill. She had thought that she wanted to die. But now, suddenly, she wanted to live. She took Fitzpiers' medicine and slowly she got better.

'My husband was a clever doctor!' Grace thought. 'Perhaps he has saved my life.'

When she was well again, Grace went to Marty South's cottage.

'We both loved Giles,' Grace said. 'Shall we visit his grave together, Marty?'

And after that, the two young women visited Giles Winterbourne's grave in the churchyard twice every week. Each time, they put flowers on the grave of the man that they had both loved.

———

So autumn passed and winter came. In February 1858, Grace received a letter from her husband. He was working in a big town, far away from Little Hintock.

> My dear Grace, my dearest wife,
>
> I think about you every day. Before I left Little Hintock, your father told me that you did not live with Giles Winterbourne. I know that you did love him then, and that you did not love me. But months have passed, my dear Grace. I am older and wiser now, and I love you more than ever.
>
> Can we meet, one day soon? I want us to be friends again.
>
> Please answer this letter.
>
> Edred

Grace agreed to meet her husband in Sherton Abbas. There was something that she wanted to know. The two young people met in the town square one afternoon.

'I have come here today for one reason,' Grace said to Fitzpiers. 'Giles Winterbourne gave me his home when I was in trouble. Then he became ill and died. I want to ask you something. Did Giles die because he gave me his home? Or did he die because he was already ill?'

'He had had typhoid. The illness had made him very weak,' Fitzpiers replied. 'You were not the cause of his death, Grace.'

'Thank you,' Grace said and she turned to leave.

'Please wait,' Fitzpiers said quietly. 'Grace, I love you more than ever before. Can you not love me a little?'

'My heart is in the grave with Giles,' Grace replied.

'Then let me meet you again as a friend,' Fitzpiers said.

Grace agreed to this. That spring, the two young people often met secretly. And soon Grace began to think that Fitzpiers had changed. He was sad and gentle, and he was kind to her. Giles Winterbourne and Felice Charmond were both dead. Could she be happy with Fitzpiers, if they lived together again?

———

One evening in early summer, Fitzpiers was waiting in a lane near Sherton Abbas. Grace was going to meet him there. Everything was very quiet. Suddenly, he heard a scream.

Fitzpiers called his wife's name. 'Grace, where are you? What has happened?'

'I'm here!' Grace called. 'I have fallen. Please help me!'

Fitzpiers ran towards his wife. He found her lying on the ground.

'My dear, dear Grace!' he said. 'Are you badly injured?'

Fitzpiers gently helped Grace to stand.

'I am sorry, Edred,' Grace said. 'I was a little late and I was running to meet you. I am not injured.'

Fitzpiers put his arms around his wife and kissed her. She did not turn away from him.

'Dearest, my aunt died and left some money for me,' Fitzpiers told her. 'I have bought a practice in the North of England. Will you come and live there with me?'

Grace did not reply but she smiled. Her husband kissed her again.

The two young people walked through the streets of the town in the bright moonlight. They soon forgot about the time. But at last Fitzpiers looked at his watch.

'There are no more trains tonight!' he exclaimed. 'I shall have to stay at a hotel. I shall stay at the 'Earl of Wessex'. Grace, please come to the hotel and stay with me.'

'But what will my parents think?' Grace said. 'They will worry about me.'

'I am sure that they will understand,' Fitzpiers said. 'People from the village have seen me here today. One of them will tell your father.'

_____

Fitzpiers was right. That evening, when Grace did not return home, George Melbury went to look for her. He soon heard about Fitzpiers. He hurried to Sherton Abbas and he asked about his daughter at the hotel.

After a short time, Grace came down the stairs.

'What are you doing here, Grace? Are you alone?' Mr Melbury asked in an angry voice.

'No,' Grace answered. 'Don't be angry, Father. I am here with Edred. He has bought a practice in the North of England. He wants me to go there with him. I have agreed.'

'Then you aren't coming home with me?' Mr Melbury asked.

'No, I will stay with my husband,' Grace replied. 'Can you understand, Father?'

'I will try to understand,' Mr Melbury said sadly. 'Good night, Grace. I am going home now.'

'Well, he *is* her husband,' George Melbury said to himself, as he rode sadly back to Lower Hintock. 'He's kissing my Grace tonight, but he'll be kissing another woman next year! Heaven knows how this story will end!'

As Melbury passed the churchyard, he saw Marty South standing alone by Giles Winterbourne's grave. He stopped his horse.

'If you're waiting for Grace, you won't see her here tonight,' Mr Melbury said. 'Mrs Fitzpiers has gone back to her husband.'

Marty did not answer. But when Melbury had gone, she knelt on the ground and put her flowers on Giles' grave.

'Now you are mine, my love,' she said quietly. 'She has forgotten you, although you died for her. But whenever I plant a tree, I will remember you, because *you* planted trees so well. While our trees grow, I will remember you, because you loved them. I will never forget you, my love. You were a good man and you did good things.'

Points for Understanding

1

1 Mr Melbury has a problem. This problem is the result of something which he did in the past. (a) Explain what this 'something' was. (b) Explain how it has made a problem for the timber-merchant.
2 Mr Percomb wants to buy Marty South's hair. At first, she refuses to sell it. But later in the chapter, she changes her mind. Why?

2

1 Mr Melbury asks Giles Winterbourne to bring Grace home from Sherton Abbas. He tells Giles that she has many new friends. Giles replies, 'I hope that she hasn't forgotten her friends from Little Hintock.' Why is Giles worried about this? Is he right to be worried?
2 Mrs Charmond lets Marty South ride on her carriage. The coachman tells Marty that this is unusual. Why do you think that Mrs Charmond lets Marty ride with her?

3

1 Mrs Charmond asks Grace about the doctor's wife. And when she sees her own reflection in the mirror, she compares her face with Grace's face, and she is not happy. What do these things tell you about Mrs Charmond?
2 Giles talks to Marty. He wants to invite a friend to a Christmas party. Marty knows who this friend is. (a) Who do you think Giles' friend is? (b) Why does he want to invite his friend to the party?

4

1 'Giles was unhappy. Everything was going wrong.' (a) What has already gone wrong for Giles at his party? (b) What else goes wrong before the end of the party?
2 Mr Melbury tells Grace to end her engagement to Giles. What are his reasons? Do you think Grace is happy about her father's decision?

5

1 Read the paper from the Hintock Hall Estate on page 32, and the letter on page 33. Why is Giles worried about his house?
2 John South dies. Doctor Fitzpiers says, 'Well, my advice has killed him!' Explain the doctor's words.

6

Giles and Fitzpiers are talking about Grace. 'Do you like her less?' Giles asks. The doctor replies, 'Well, perhaps I like her a little less.' Why does he say this? What does this conversation tell you about Fitzpiers? Find some other sentences in this chapter which tell you the same thing.

7

1 What happens every year, at midnight, on Midsummer's Eve?
2 Grace 'knew that Fitzpiers was clever, but she did not like some of his ideas'. Which ideas do you think Grace dislikes?

8

'A girl from the village came to me very early this morning. She had a terrible toothache,' says Fitzpiers. Why does Fitzpiers not tell Grace the girl's name? What does Fitzpiers' answer tell you about his story? Do you think that his story is true?

9

1 Mrs Charmond has asked Fitzpiers to visit her. She says that she has had an accident in her carriage. Do you think that she has another reason for asking the doctor to come?
2 'Now I have spoilt your career,' Mrs Charmond says to Fitzpiers. What does she mean by this?

10

1 Mrs Charmond asks Marty about Giles. 'Are you engaged to him?' she asks. Why do you think that she asks this question?

2 Marty gives Fitzpiers a letter which tells him about Mrs Charmond's hair. Why do you think that Marty tells the doctor this secret?

3 'I shall never be free, unless —' Fitzpiers says. What do you think the rest of this sentence was going to be?

11

'I will be free very soon,' Grace tells Giles. Why does she think this?

12

1 'I have killed you, Giles! I have killed you!' Grace says. Why does she say this?

2 Grace tells Fitzpiers a lie – she says that she has been Giles' lover. Why do you think that she says this?

13

1 Grace agrees to meet her husband in Sherton Abbas. (a) What is the reason that she gives him? (b) Do you think that she has another reason?

2 At the end of the story, Marty South is alone at Giles' grave. 'You were a good man and you did good things,' she says. Do you think that Marty is right?

3 Which person in the book do you think behaves best?

Glossary

1 **oaks, elms, ashes, hazels** (page 5)
these are all kinds of trees that grow in woodlands in Britain. The leaves of these trees fall from the branches in the autumn. In the spring, new green leaves grow on the trees again.

Other trees that are mentioned in the story are: *apple* (page 5), *fir* (page 22), *holly* (page 22). *Apple trees* are grown in gardens and in large fields called *orchards*. The fruit of apple trees is good to eat. *Fir trees*, *holly trees* and *ivy plants* (page 19) have dark green leaves. The leaves stay on the branches all the year.

Woodlanders work in woods and forests. These men and women look after the trees and they cut them down to make things from the *timber*. They also plant new, young trees. These areas of new trees are called *plantations*.

The timber from different trees is used for different things. For example, the wood from the trunks of oak trees is used for boats, furniture and strong wooden tools. The branches of hazel trees are used to make *thatched roofs* for houses (see Glossary 4, below). The rough *bark* from the trunks of trees is used when leather is prepared.

2 *living* – *earnt their living* (page 5)

the people lived in the woodlands. They looked after the trees. They sold the timber to earn money.

3 *hurdles* (page 5)

thin hazel branches are pushed together to make a strong, flat piece of fence called a *hurdle*. Many hurdles are joined together to keep farm animals in one area.

4 *thatching* (page 5)

a *thatch* is a roof of a house that is made of the leaves and stems of long plants. *Thatching* is the way that the leaves are held together. The thatch is held on the roof of the house by *spars* – long thin pieces of strong hazel wood. The spars are pushed down across the leaves. A thatch keeps the inside of the house dry when the weather is wet and cold. It keeps the inside of the house cool when the weather is hot.

5 *shillings* (page 6)

British money at the time of this story was pounds (£), shillings (s) and pence (d). Shilling coins were made of silver. 20 shillings = one pound. A *sovereign* (page 8) was a gold coin. One sovereign = one pound.

6 *hair-piece* (page 6)

a long piece of hair that is worn on the head. Women wear *hair-pieces* to make their own hair-style longer and thicker. At the time of this story, the hair for hair-pieces often came from poor women who sold it for money.

7 *going abroad* (page 6)

leaving Britain to travel to other countries.

8 *Hintock House Estate* (page 6)

the *estate* is the land around Hintock House – the largest house in the village of Little Hintock. This land is woodlands, fields and plantations. It is owned by the person who lives in Hintock House. The owner of the estate also owns many buildings on the estate. See Glossary 10, below.

9 **blushed** (page 8)

Marty is uncomfortable about this conversation. Her face has become red.

10 **leases** (page 8)

are legal agreements between the owners of houses and the people who live in the houses. The document says who may live there and for how many years. *Lifeholds* are special leases that continue while the person who is named on the document is alive.

11 **bundles** (page 9)

many pieces of wood are tied together in a *bundle*.

12 **reflection** (page 10)

when you look at a mirror, you see a picture of yourself. This is your *reflection*.

13 **bonnet** (page 11)

a woman's hat.

14 **tree-planter and cider-maker** (page 12)

Giles earns money in two ways. He is a *tree-planter* – he works in the woodlands. He plants new young trees in the ground and looks after them as they grow. He is also a *cider-maker*. Farmers who have apple trees bring the ripe apples to Giles in the autumn. At this time, the fruit is sweet. Giles puts the apples in a large machine which presses the fruit. The sweet juice comes out of the apples and an alcoholic drink – *cider* – is made from it.

15 **gig** (page 12)

a small carriage that is pulled by one horse. The person who owned the gig usually drove it. Large *carriages* were pulled by two or four horses. Carriages were owned by richer people. A carriage-driver, or coachman, drove the carriage. *Wagons* were large wooden vehicles pulled by many horses. Wagons were used on farms and also in towns. Every kind of thing could be carried on a wagon. They had large wheels and were very heavy. There were no cars or trucks at this time. People rode on horses or they travelled in vehicles pulled by horses. Steam trains ran on metal railway lines. People travelled on trains for longer journeys. They crossed seas in steamships.

16 **experiments in his laboratory** (page 17)

Doctor Fitzpiers is a clever and well-educated man. He is more interested in studying science than looking after patients who are ill. He has a room in his house where he studies. The room has books and pieces of scientific equipment. It is a *laboratory*. Fitzpiers studies how human bodies work. When he is studying, he makes *experiments* (or tests) on parts of bodies.

17 *at ease* – *to feel at ease* (page 17)
feel happy and comfortable because you like the place where you
are and the people that you are with.

18 *examine* (page 18)
look at, or study, carefully. Doctors *examine* patients who are feel
ing ill.

19 *hollow* (page 19)
an area of land that is lower than the ground around it.

20 *good society* (page 24)
the words *good society* were used to describe wealthy and well-
educated people. Rich people in *good society* owned large houses
and a lot of property. They travelled to many different places and
they knew about art, literature and science.

21 *bakehouse* (page 25)
a small building which contained a large oven. Bread and dishes of
meat were cooked in bakehouses because the kitchens of houses
were small.

22 *cleaning and polishing the furniture* (page 25)
the boy has come to Giles' house to clean the house before the
party. He has rubbed polish onto the furniture. The polish makes
the wooden furniture shine.

23 *frowned* (page 26)
Mr Melbury is angry when Creedle spills the food on Grace. His
eyebrows move down towards his eyes. This movement is called
frowning.

24 *tell the young woman's fortune* (page 26)
the old woman was going to talk to Grace. Perhaps she was also
going to look at her hands. Then she would tell Grace what was
going to happen to her in the future.

25 *sighed* (page 27)
a soft noise that Mr Melbury makes because he is worried or
unhappy.

26 *ladder* (page 29)
a piece of equipment which is used to climb up to high places. *Ladders*
are made from two long poles joined together with bars. You stand on
these bars.

27 *saw* (page 29)
a metal tool which is used to cut wood.

28 *passed to* (page 32)
when Mrs Winterbourne died, all the properties, documents and
money that she owned were given to her husband. They were now
his. That was the law.

29 **pity** – *to pity* (page 34)
feel sad for someone who has been unlucky or unhappy.

30 **hayfield** (page 46)
hay is long dried grass which is fed to animals. A *hayfield* is a field where the grass is specially grown to make hay.

31 **cough** (page 46)
a noise that you make in your throat when your mouth is dry, or if you are ill.

32 **buy a practice** (page 49)
a *practice* is a doctor's business. In Britain at this time, people who were ill paid doctors to look after them. The government did not pay doctors for their work. Medicines were not free. When a doctor stopped working, he sold his business – his practice – to another doctor. A new doctor had to *buy a practice* before he could look after patients in an area.

33 **registry office** (page 49)
an official building where people can get married.

34 **toll ticket** (page 60)
at the time of this story, people had to pay the government when they travelled on some roads in Britain. Gates were built across these roads in special places. The gates were called turnpikes. A man worked in a small building at the turnpike. He stopped all the travellers on the road. They gave him some money. Then he gave them a toll ticket and opened the gate.

35 **reins** (page 69)
a rider uses these thin leather straps to stop the horse, or to make it turn to the left or the right.

36 **divorce law** (page 75)
when two people want to finish their marriage they get a *divorce*. They go to a court and ask for a legal paper which says that their marriage has finished. Before 1857, people in Britain were not able to get a divorce easily. Men and women were married to each other until one of them died. In 1857, the British law was changed. After this, a man or a woman could get divorced if a judge agreed with them.

37 **typhoid** (page 81)
a dangerous illness which passes from one person to another very easily.

Published by Macmillan Heinemann ELT
Between Towns Road, Oxford, OX4 3PP
Macmillan Heinemann ELT is an imprint of
Macmillan Publishers Limited
Companies and representatives throughout the world

ISBN 0 333 75799 8

This retold version for Macmillan Guided Readers
First published 1999
Text © Margaret Tarner 1999, 2001, 2003
Design and illustration © Macmillan Publishers Limited 1999, 2001, 2003
Heinemann is a registered trademark of Reed Educational & Professional Publishing Limited
This version first published 2003

Illustrated by Alexy Pendle
Cover photo by Liam Daniel from
"The Woodlanders", Channel Four Films/Pathé Productions Limited.
Cover design by Marketplace Design

Printed in China

2007 2006 2005 2004 2003
12 11 10 9 8 7 6 5 4 3